THE FINAL FLAW

BOOK DESIGN BY Ivica Jandrijevic
COVER ILLUSTRATION BY Henry Relf

ISBN

979-8-9859296-0-7 *Paperback*
979-8-9859296-1-4 *eBook*

FIRST EDITION. APRIL 2022

THIS IS A WORK OF FICTION.

All characters in this publication are fictitious. Any resemblance to a
living or dead person, business or companies is entirely coincidental.

michaelrsullivan.com

THE
FINAL FLAW

MICHAEL
R. SULLIVAN

Dedicated to our flaws and imperfections,
the source of all beauty in this world.

CHAPTER 1

———

My neck spasmed. The tics building up with the slow inevitability of a thunderstorm looming towards the city. I paced back and forth in the hallway, running over the words I'd rehearsed so many times before. Expensive shoes squeaked on the floor in front of the stage, the lobby doors swung open and closed. Each sound was another person to judge my every word.

Every movement.

Every twitch.

Each time a tic came on I ignored it, hoping they might pass. They never did. The left half of my neck convulsed, my eyes snapped shut. I fought them, pretending they wouldn't get worse. I imagined the speech going smoothly, the words flowing out of my mouth and the crowd hanging on every word. Closing my eyes, I breathed in deeply, attempting to relax my body. I seized. There was no stopping them, I'd never been able to turn my tics off before, but a part of me hoped that might finally change.

My body felt like a jerking marionette outside of my own control.

The noise from the audience seeped through the door frame. I heard the murmurs of the crowd, the shifting of chairs as people positioned themselves in the room. The moment was here and there was no wishing away what I was.

The door to the stage room opened. James poked his head through, his dark features shadowed by the dim lights in the auditorium behind him. "You're on in two minutes."

I nodded. Unsure if words could form in my mouth.

"You can do this, we all believe in you," James said, standing in the doorway, half in and half out, wearing a light grey suit. He looked like he wanted to say more, but he didn't. He gave me a tight-lipped smile and left. There was concern in his eyes, he knew how challenging this next part would be. The door closed behind him leaving me alone with my thoughts in the hallway.

Again, I ticced. Each time bringing me back to the reality of what was to come. Alone they didn't bother me, but standing on stage with hundreds of eyes watching my every movement, each tic served as another reminder of how strange I looked to others. This wasn't my skill set, my place was behind a computer screen, not in front of a crowd.

My heartbeat pulsed, the warm air of the hallway thick around me. The world was changing, and I had an opportunity to do something about it. I twitched again, this time letting the feeling fall into the background, I wouldn't let them control me. Not now.

The commotion and talk softened when I walked through the door, the auditorium seemed larger as less sound bounced around its dimly lit walls. I felt their eyes immediately, no judgment in them yet, just curiosity. I walked past members of the board, the exact people I needed to impress. The system seemed flawed, such a small group of people held such a large amount of power. They claimed to have no bias, but their scanning eyes didn't feel impartial.

Their vote would decide what made it into the Template, the genetic future of millions controlled by twenty people. Some wore suits, others lab coats, but everyone held themselves with an air of prestige.

My neck spasmed again as I climbed the stairs to the stage, but I couldn't dwell on my physical body. I saw Gerhard as I scanned the room. He sat in his electric wheelchair, rather than one of the auditorium seats. The most powerful man at Mendelium, his attention solely on me.

I ticced. The pulse from my neck running through my entire arm.

If anyone here understood what it was to be different it was him. With no legs and only a partial right arm, his distinguished face was perched atop a fragmented body. As always, the wheelchair seemed like an extension of his physique. Today his face—the one plastered to screens and billboards throughout the city—focused on me.

I squinted as the stage lights beamed into my face. Taking my place behind the podium, my hands planted on the thick wood panels. I straightened my glasses then looked out across the sea of people before me. Hundreds more than I expected.

My neck contracted again, right on cue, and the self-doubt creeped in. The stress charged through me, each second feeling longer as time compressed. I scanned the crowd, clearing my throat into the microphone.

Elizabeth sat near the front, her golden blonde hair, flowing over her shoulder. She had a soft reassuring smile on her face, the same smile she wore when she'd encouraged me this morning, the same smile as the day we first met. I could do this.

"My name is Charlie Lamarck," I said, my words reverberating across the crowd. "I'm here today because I'm different. I'm strange. Tourette's syndrome isn't conducive to social interactions and my tics are distracting to other people. As the Template matures, we increase life expectancy and remove dangerous diseases from the gene pool. This is revolutionary for people with birth defects, but I am not one of those people.

"The jerking and nervous blinking is part of who I am. Each day is a battle against my own body, the constant urge to convulse is completely outside the control of my conscious mind. It is a battle I lose, but one I choose to fight. Constantly suppressing tics relies on the activation of the dorsolateral prefrontal cortex. A big name for a tiny area of the brain tied to self-control and working memory. Brain scans have revealed this area to be substantially larger in people with Tourette's syndrome.

"I tell you this so you understand why I stand in front of you today. Years of fighting against my own body have molded me into what I am. My disadvantages turned into advantages, the act of overcoming the tics has physically transformed my mind. I've enjoyed success in life, not in spite of the struggle, but *because of the struggle.*

"People with Tourette's syndrome score higher in self-control and spend more time in flow states. These facts get ignored because our tics make others uncomfortable. I urge you to open your minds and hear the opinion of someone who has suffered from the affliction you wish to eliminate.

"Removing something from the Template is final— forever gone from the collective human genome. We barely understand the implications of the disorder, yet there are thousands of people like me who believe their symptoms bring more richness to their lives. We are not worse, just different.

I plead to you today to continue the investigation; I'm only asking for more time."

CHAPTER 2

———

My coworkers moved around the sprawling dining room. Their eyes avoided me, looking instead to the ornate woodwork lining the edges of the room or the crystal chandeliers above. *Twitchy. Blinky. Spaz.*

I heard the names I'd been called so many times before, echoes from my past regurgitated into the present. I felt as alienated now as I had in my youth. The goal of the speech was to influence change, but the board voted unanimously against my proposal.

The people seated around me weren't talking about genetic research or this year's Template. Most were brown nosing with their bosses or sales teams putting on a show for clients. I didn't have stories of traveling to international branches and rubbing shoulders with big names in the industry. Writing code would always be better than socializing and small talk.

I looked across the mingling crowds to the only person in the room not shooting me a glare—Elizabeth. My wife, who normally balanced out my complete distaste for small talk, paced along the other side of the ballroom. She looked beautiful tonight, wearing the confidence of someone who was good at their job. She pointed directions to the waiting staff and gave a smile to the passing guests. Her voice echoed through my head.

You do know the point of a party is to talk to people right Charlie?

I threw back the last of my drink and stood. She was busy, but—as usual—she was right. I started over towards the bar hoping to grab another drink and find someone who didn't act allergic to me. I ticced, they always seemed to be worse when I drank. Alcohol put to sleep the portion of my mind that helped with self-control, the constant watcher was gone. *I suppose that's the point.*

"There he is," said a booming voice from behind me. The overpowering smell of cologne hit me before his words did and I struggled not to cringe. "Your wife throws one hell of a party."

"Hey Dave."

"Charlie, Charlie, Charlie," he began with a slur in his voice, "I don't know how in the hell a twitchy little man like you scored a woman like that."

I didn't respond.

Over his shoulder towards the bar, a few of the other board member's eyes darted away. They sat in a booth surrounded by tables of people hoping to rub shoulders with the most powerful people at Mendelium. It wasn't my game, the people here specialized in swapping names and climbing career ladders.

"I'll tell you what," he said, his words slurred, "if I had a woman like that I would make—"

"How is your wife doing these days, Dave?" I interjected.

"She's at home watching the kids," he said to me wearing a smug look, teetering slightly side to side.

"Didn't want to bring them out to party with you and your drinking buddies?"

He took an intentional step in closer to me, planting his hairy hand on my shoulder. His flushed cheeks matched the red in his bloodshot eyes.

"Listen to me closely Charlie, cause I'm about to give you some of the best advice you are ever liable to receive."

A hand grabbed onto his shoulder, and he let go of me, looking over to his side. He stumbled back as he did it, "...there's the life of the party!"

He threw his arm around James' shoulder and pulled him into our conversation, his glare turned into a hollow smile.

"Hey Dave," James smiled, looking as put together as ever. He wore a brilliant blue tie that contrasted his fitted grey suit. Seeing him made me question my own relaxed attire, "Enjoying yourself?"

"You know I am," Dave said, his words slurring into each other. "Where's your drink?"

"Charlie here owes me one," he said, giving me a wink.

Dave didn't say anything, he shot me another glare and turned back to James who watched his gesture with a smirk on his face.

"Tell you what," Dave said, focusing carefully not to trip over his words, "after you're done why don't you come swing over and chat with me and the rest of the board. You and I have something to discuss."

"Sure," James beamed and patted Dave on the shoulder as he walked away. *How did he always make social interactions seem so easy?*

"What exactly do I owe you a drink for?" I asked James as Dave walked away.

"One—for getting you away from that idiot, and two—your wife just transferred me some money and told me I need to do something about you moping over here all by yourself."

He led the way towards the bar.

We walked past Dave's table, they quieted as James and I passed.

"You don't seem too popular tonight," he said with a smirk.

I rolled my eyes at him. "Shouldn't you be talking up some clients or doing the rounds?"

"Nah, you're my priority tonight, C, do you want to head around back, grab some food?" he asked.

"I don't know, did Liz give you *permission* to take me away from the party?"

He gave me a deadpan stare. "I saw you earlier. You weren't exactly a social butterfly before, and your stock has fallen. I'm a bit surprised Mendelium still hired Elizabeth to plan this party after your speech."

"Liz said they didn't know we're married until after they hired her, if they knew she wouldn't have gotten the contract."

James flashed a smile, but I could see a hint of pity in his eyes. I saw that look too frequently these days.

"I brought this upon myself," I said, "Come on, I've got a drink for you."

We walked through the bar and out the doors onto the patio area. The warm night air and traffic sounds of the city hit me as we passed through. The lights were dimmer out here, we stood near the railing overlooking the square in front of Mendelium Tower's entrance. Self-driving cars pulsed down the streets in synchronicity, all of them moving like a single interconnected organism. The lights of the surrounding city so bright the moon was barely noticeable.

"Have you been busy tonight?" I asked.

"You could say that." James said, "There's a party out there, and that's the best way to meet new clientele."

"You call them clientele?" I questioned with a smile, "Seems like a drug dealer should call them addicts or something."

"Whoa, whoa, whoa," James said raising his palms, "You know I hate that term—I'm simply a guy with a talent for procuring things."

"Illegal things."

"Occasionally. Look C, I'm an upstanding citizen," he adjusted his grey blazer and straightened his tie for effect, "I don't do anything unethical; I'm helping people get what they already want. I'm a middleman. Just think of how good a role model I am for young men; they can aspire to be a high-end drug dealer to the hyper-successful elites of the world."

"You and I are very different people," I said to him, leaning against the patio railing, looking out over the moving crowds of people walking on the sidewalks below.

"I wouldn't have it any other way," he said.

"If you were in my shoes and people were talking about you behind your back you would walk straight up to them and say something about it."

"Not a chance I would ever be in your shoes. I'm not audacious enough to claim that a neurological disorder is a good thing to a board of people whose entire job is removing genetic imperfections from the world."

"Not my brightest idea," I said, as I pushed up my glasses on my nose.

James put his elbows on the railing and leaned in towards me lowering his voice slightly. "Feeling like an outcast must be draining. You might get some pressure from Gerhard or the board, but at the end of the day, you spoke your mind. No one can ever take that from you."

"You don't *change* the Template with a few well-rehearsed words," I began, "just because some Tourettic guy got up in front of people and gave a speech doesn't mean it's going to impact their decision. I made no difference. I can't stop human nature James; this train is on its path and there is no slowing it down.

"Stop that Charlie," James said. "When things mattered, you stepped up to that podium and spoke your piece. I respect that. The world has enough figureheads, enough people who can smile nice and say the things everyone else wants to hear. You need to have more faith in yourself, your voice is important."

"The board voted, and things are moving forward, I used what little pull I had and I fell short."

"You did all you could," James said. "You can't focus too much on the outcome. You did the right thing."

"Thanks James." I said, contracting my neck in an involuntary tic.

James stared at me for a moment.

"What do they feel like?" he asked, "I don't mean to be rude, but they are something that makes up your entire life, I've always wondered what you experience?"

I looked around the restaurant, dark wood rafters lined the patio above. "Imagine a spider fell on you from up there, right onto the back of your neck. You wouldn't think about it. You'd react. Something instinctual happens, overriding conscious thought. Whenever I tic, it's sort of like that. My body reacts and my brain doesn't process what happened until afterwards.

"With practice you learn to delay them a bit, but every inch the spider crawls over your skin the primal urge to swipe it away grows stronger. Eventually it builds up and your willpower breaks. You swat it away."

"Can you ever control them?" he asked.

"No more than you can control the urge to shiver when you step outside into the cold. Maybe I can hold back for a moment or two, but it's going to happen. It's better to embrace them and let them flow through me rather than fighting against them constantly."

The patio door opened, behind us as a couple more party guests stepped outside. A loud scream echoed from the restaurant. James shot me a concerned look, the two of us ran back inside.

"What's going on?" James asked the waitstaff as we walked towards the ballroom. They didn't answer. Everyone around shared confused looks and apprehensively moved toward the commotion. The screams continued as we walked closer, passing by the bar, the seats now empty. There was a crowd gathered in the center of the room, people craning their necks and looking towards what was happening at the interior of the ballroom. Someone hit my shoulder as they ran past.

A paramedic.

I looked around the room, scanning the back wall where I saw Liz earlier. She wasn't there. A shot of cold adrenaline spread through me, the hair stood up on my arms. I scanned the entire room again, frantically shoving my way through the crowd, the angry grumbles of those I ran into sounded distant. She was here a moment ago, not far from where the paramedics now gathered. *What if something had happened?* I tried to push the thought from my mind, but the tension of the crowd brought it right back. I ticced then, my eyes snapping shut, anxiety mounting.

As I neared the center of the group, arms wrapped around my side nearly knocking me over. It was her. I reciprocated the hug, her loose blonde curls falling into my face the smell of her hair feeling so warm in the room of cold stares.

"He—he just collapsed," Liz said. There was so much worry in her eyes, but I didn't care. She was safe.

We moved through the crowd, her hand in mine with no intention of letting go. The music stopped, the sound of murmurs reverberating through the room. The paramedics hunched over a collapsed body on the floor.

"There is nothing more we can do," one paramedic whispered to the other, looking defeated.

A large man lay on the floor, there was vomit splattered around him and covering the lab coat of one of the board members. A hairy forearm hung limp at his side. I smelled his overpowering cologne as Liz and I approached the circle.

CHAPTER 3

———

THREE YEARS EARLIER

I looked past the reception desk, out across the city. From the ninety-third floor I could see the tops of the surrounding buildings. Not so long ago I'd looked up here and envisioned a better life for me and my employees.

Mendelium Tower epitomized the future, building better humans through science and innovation. We now had everything I thought we wanted, but it wasn't all what it seemed. There was an emptiness here, I could feel it in this metallic waiting room. We lost something. I'd sold out.

All their false promises about the partnership became clear, they saw us as dollar signs. They didn't care about the team we'd created or the culture and products we'd grown. We were simply the newest cogs in their monolithic machine. I'd always imagined working at Mendelium would be meaningful. What better cause was there than eliminating genetic diseases from future generations? If I threw myself into the work and solved the problems that needed solving, we would be rewarded for our efforts. I was naive.

I walked into the room; board members clustered across the long oak table. The skyline of the city outlining their expensive dresses and suits. These weren't my people, they carried themselves with an affluence I couldn't imitate. I adjusted my tie. I hated wearing the thing and the suit accompanying it. Nothing about it made me work better, nothing about it made my mind solve better problems or craft better code. I would have to jump through these hoops for the time being, I would wear what they wanted me to wear. Things would change, but first I had to bide my time.

"You must be Charlie," said a heavy-set man, extending a large hairy hand. "I'm Dave Lattimore, it's a pleasure to have you aboard."

"Thank you," I said trying to smile at each of the board members in turn. I saw their cautious glances, closely examining everything from my dress to my mannerisms.

"From what I hear, you are the brains behind Geni-Sense, it's wonderful to meet you."

"I'm one of the *many* brains behind GeniSense, we are... or were, a close-knit team. We may have been small, but we used our small size as an advantage, maneuvering in ways companies like Mendelium could not. I supposed that's why you stopped competing and decided to buy us out."

"Pretty fat check," Dave said, "hope you bought something fun with it."

I bit my lip and nodded, "I was hoping we could talk about what is happening to my employees. Many of them are being let go."

"It's unfortunate, but the reality is the most valuable part of GeniSense was your technology and security systems. We appreciate everything you've built, but it doesn't make sense for the company to keep all of them on, our team here is top of the line, we—"

"I've been responsible for those people's lives for the last four years," I said, attempting to exude as much confidence as possible. "Do you understand what that means? I've made promises to each of their faces, to their *families*. We deliberated for months if we should sell to Mendelium, I finally decided it was the best for everyone. We could ensure payment for their years of hard work. I promised them, just as I was promised by many of you, that we would continue operating as a team. You can't just fire them."

"They will be given generous severance packages," Dave said, "I assure you they will be compensated fairly."

"This is about more than money." I shot back, "We were a *team*, we built GeniSense together."

The rage bubbled up inside me, my words louder than I intended. The talking around the table stopped.

"...Are you alright?" Dave asked, looking at me oddly.

"I'm frustrated. I was lied to. By Gerhard and by each and every one of you. Every day I've been here something more is taken away, I didn't know signing a dotted line would negatively impact those people's lives. This is my own fault; I made a promise to each of them and failed. I came here because it's not right, and I need some answers."

"That's not what I meant," Dave said, "your arm keeps jerking."

"Are you having a seizure?" Asked one of the female board members, she brushed her red hair over her shoulder looking on at me with a concerned gaze.

"No, I'm fine," I said. "I have to explain to these people why they are losing their jobs, I gave them my word and now they look at me wondering what is happening."

"Just relax for a moment, it looks serious," she said again. "I think we should call for a medic, I knew someone who was having a seizure, but didn't—"

"No," I yelled back, again letting my anger come untethered. "I have Tourette's syndrome, the arm jerking is just a tic, it gets worse when I'm stressed out."

"Oh," she said, "I'm so sorry"

"It looks painful," said another man in the back of the room.

I was now acutely aware of the continued spasms of my right arm, distracting from what I came in here to say. Why did stress always have to cause it? Did it always have to happen during pivotal moments of my life?

Dave paused, "Are you going to be alright?"

I could see a shift in them, a change in the way they regarded me. I morphed from human to zoo animal, something new, a curiosity to observe rather than someone whose opinion held value. I hated this moment. The momentum behind my words was lost, the thoughts I carried into the room, the faces of my employees I was fighting for fell away. I felt embarrassed, not about the tics, but how I was letting down all the people I came to fight for. They deserved a better leader, someone who could get them their jobs back.

"You must be so thrilled to work here." the woman said, "That's one of the traits we are considering removing with the Template, you can prevent future generations from going through the pain and frustration you have. We hope to make conditions like yours a thing of the past."

"Too bad we can't do anything for you right now," said Dave, no longer meeting my eyes but staring at my thrashing arm. "It's so distracting."

CHAPTER 4

————

"We might have a couple summer days left after all," I said to Liz. Columns of morning light poured through the windows across our kitchen table, reflecting papers and work Liz had strewn across its surface. It was a struggle getting out of bed this morning, but these small moments with my wife to start the day always lightened my mood.

Liz sat perched at the counter reading an article, the smell of coffee greeting me before her smile. "Did you learn any more about Dave?"

The smile left her face and she looked up at me, "No. Nothing. I wish there was something we could do for his family. I feel terrible Charlie, I've never had something like that happen at one of my parties before. I feel responsible."

"That's not on you, Liz. Your guests had an excellent time last night. Just because it happened during your event doesn't mean you shoulder the blame."

"We still don't know," she said leaning against the counter. Her arms crossed, her braided hair hanging over her shoulder. "It could have been something he ate, if so, it was my fault. We should have been monitoring people more closely, what if the paramedics could have been there faster? No matter how I see this some of the blame lands on me. When people attend one of my events it's my duty to look out for their best interests. They are trusting me with their time."

I noticed the bags under her eyes and the coffee she was nursing. "Did you sleep last night?"

She turned away from me, grabbing her breakfast plate and walking towards the sink, "No."

"You aren't going back into work this morning, are you?"

"I have to."

"You do not," I said. "Elizabeth, you need rest."

"That isn't a luxury I have at the moment," she said through her teeth, washing the plate with more pressure than it needed.

I walked up behind her, placing my hands on her shoulders, I could feel the tension in her muscles. She turned around, her blue eyes bloodshot, and she hugged me. Her damp hands soaking through my shirt, we stood there briefly, her head against my chest.

"We are one hell of a pair right now," she said with a laugh. "Let's take a vacation after things settle down a little bit, a weekend away, just you and me."

"I would love that, with everything going on lately the office no longer feels welcoming. Getting away for a little would probably do everyone some good."

An alarm went off and she pressed a button to stop it.

"Don't let them pressure you Charlie, you spoke your piece and they ignored you. Remember, they are only doing what they think is best for the world."

"And they're wrong."

"They are, but I have to go," she said while smiling and grabbing her bags. "I hope your day will be less hectic than mine is about to be."

I stood up to grab her arm and pulled her in for a kiss before she left. I organized my things and poured myself a cup of coffee into a mug for my commute, it was a small piece of home to bring with me today. Living in the city had its perks, riding the metro was one of them. The noise and hustle of the city was so different from the small town I grew up in, but there were parts I appreciated. Surrounded by hundreds of strangers my tics weren't as noticeable. I was just another twitchy guy on the train, one more crazy person in the sea of psychos.

The people on the subway pulsed around me, I was the water that flowed past them, trying as best I could to blend in. Next to me sat a mother and a young boy with a backpack in his arms. He looked around the car with adventurous eyes. The subway that blended into the background of my day was completely new to him, the doors and lights each a new thing to experience. He looked in my direction and I became acutely aware of my right hand. Twitching. Extending my fingers and twisting my wrist, it wasn't enough to just tense my neck, this morning my tics were strong from a lack of sleep last night. He looked at me confused.

My generation would be one of the last to live through the randomness of natural born genetics.

He probably didn't know what the Template was, or how much pain and suffering it potentially saved him from, yet his entire life was shaped by it. His mother sitting next to him almost certainly wore a Template device during her conception and pregnancy. Everyone did. Why take a risk with your child's future when you could constantly monitor every physical metric to you to ensure your child is developing optimally?

He smiled watching the platforms and buildings flash by, with the childlike ignorance for the problems most of us suffered. His generation would never truly understand my struggles, they would never know the pain so many of us went through. The sacrifices we'd made to ensure they grew up in comfortable lives.

The mother and child got off and I exited the station at the next stop. The cool breeze jolted me awake despite the bright sunshine hanging in the early morning sky. I grabbed two bagels from a food stall as I walked the final few blocks towards the office. Taking a bite did me good, there was still a lingering feeling of anxiety from last night. *Dave was dead.* I hadn't heard anything from the initial police reports but knowing him it was probably an overdose of some kind.

Mendelium Tower stood in the distance, the gigantic double-helix shaped building grew taller with each block. Like a monolithic twisting ladder, it spiraled up to it's peak over two-thousand feet above. As I crossed the street towards the pavilion the clouds reflected off the black mirror-like sides. People of the city complained about it initially—claiming the futuristic look tarnished the city skyline—but I disagreed.

Mendelium created world changing technology, it was fitting that our building looked like a gigantic strand of DNA reaching up towards the sky above instead of just another lifeless grey rectangle.

Mendelium Tower represented the future, it represented endless potential. Genetic manipulation wasn't simply a way to improve people's lives, it would change the entire trajectory of our species.

I wanted to see it go down the right path.

Outcroppings expanded over each side of the building, hanging gardens hundreds of feet above the rest of the skyline. The left of which I'd had the chance to visit during dinner parties hosted by the company. The right accessible only through the executive rooms near Gerhard's office.

Commuters moved across the square in front of the entry way. A giant marble fountain stood in the center with a mob of protesters standing at its side. Their aggressive signs and chants were just as much part of my commute as the ride on the metro. No matter how widespread the Template had become it always seemed like there were a few people who thought we were undermining the natural world.

Entering the building felt like any other day. I slid through the glass doors, immune to the beauty of the ornately decorated ceiling. It was easy to recognize those who hadn't been inside before. Their eyes gawking above as I dodged my way around them moving towards security. *There were more people than usual.*

Across the sprawling first floor of Mendelium Tower people crowded towards a makeshift stage. A press conference must be underway. Gerhard Geller sat in his wheelchair on stage, the noise of the security checkpoints masked any of his words. The short security guard with liver spots scattered across his wrinkled skin smiled at me as I walked past the line.

"Morning Li," I said, handing him the other bagel I bought, "I got the usual for you. What's going on here this morning?"

"Thanks Mr. Lamarck," he said, a small spark flashing in his eye as he broke the routine of checking bags for security threats. "Just another press conference. Something about the incident last night from the bits I've heard."

"You've got to stop calling me that," I said, "I'm just Charlie."

"No can-do Mr. Lamarck, old habits die hard," he said setting the bagel down then starting to unwrap it. "You were my boss for four of the best years of my life, if GeniSense didn't take a chance and hire me I don't know where my family and I would be today."

"Three years Li."

"It feels like it was longer," he said, taking a bite and nodding kindly at me.

I smiled, but it hurt hearing about the past. Had selling to Mendelium actually improved his life? All our old coworkers had been fired in the months after the acquisition, Li and I were the only two GeniSense employees remaining. The mind-numbing security job he had now looked a lot less enviable than security and maintenance back at GeniSense. I still felt I let him down, hopefully some warm food from a friendly face would improve his day.

"Life moves fast in this building," Li said, "I don't hear much over here, they just have me check bags and look pretty, but Dave's death has been the talk of the crowd."

I nodded at him. "Have a good rest of your day," I said, then gave him the most genuine smile I could muster this early in the morning.

Rather than heading towards the elevator I found a place to stand near the back of the crowd. As I approached, I could begin to hear Gerhard's well practiced speaking voice.

"—so unfortunate." Gerhard continued, shaking his head, "He was an incredible member of our team and a close friend of mine. Dave Lattimore will be deeply missed by all of us at Mendelium."

I smiled at Gerhard's kind words in memoriam of Dave, but beneath it was guilt. I felt the sorrow of the crowd around me, but I couldn't relate. This was the man who openly mocked me on every occasion he got. I didn't want him to die, but it didn't feel wrong either. *Did that make me a bad person?*

His wife Cynthia was in tears near the front of the stage. She wore a dark blue dress, more somber than her normally bright and colorful clothing choices. It contrasted with her light features, making her seem ghostlike. Seeing her in this state—tears running down her cheeks—hit something in me. My personal opinions of the man aside, he was close to many people, a part of their life was gone.

"His jokes could make anyone laugh, his golf game legendary, and his work ethic renowned. I respected him deeply, and I hope his memory will live inside of all of us." Gerhard spoke from the podium with a look of genuine sadness on his face. Even from his wheelchair, he commanded a presence on the stage.

"Dave sacrificed so much for this company. He dedicated his life to the pursuit of improving future generations. In remembrance, Mendelium has made a sizable donation to his family to help them navigate through this difficult time," Gerhard's words didn't sound practiced, though they likely were. He commanded the stage as his voice echoed out across the gigantic entryway into the ears of employees and reporters. "His passing will affect our operations here permanently. Though we will never fully fill in or replace someone as critical to our operations as Dave, we still plan to hit this year's Template deadline on time."

Back to business. Time to focus on the upcoming deadline. No matter how much they talked of memories and a life well lived, the reality hung right in front of us. This was a job, any delays would affect millions of families relying on our product.

"Replacing Dave is no simple task; his attitude and personality were a positive influence on so many of us. But the Template affects millions of people across the world, so our work must move on. Because of this we've come to a fast decision to fill our newest member of the board. In Dave's stead, longtime partner Charlie Lamarck will be taking his place. Charlie is currently the Director of Distributed Computing, his resume consists of founding a—" the words faded as I recognized my name. I heard murmurs near me, a few people stared in my direction. I became acutely aware of my body, and how far down my jaw was hanging. It took all my willpower to hide the traces of fear from my face, but the surprise surely stayed. *How could they pick me? No one asked.*

Right then I wanted to run away from the crowd, I attempted to flash a knowing smile to those around me who were looking in my direction. I stood; my feet fixated to the cold granite floor I attempted to look natural while the situation unfolded. My tics pulsed every few seconds. Gerhard finished his speech and left the stage. I wanted so badly to confront him, but in my current state of emotions figured it best to wait. James walked towards me, deliberately dodging his way through the crowd.

"What the hell C?" he said, his face mixed with excitement and confusion. "Why wouldn't you tell me?"

"I didn't know. If I would have been in early to work this morning, I would have walked straight past this and not found out at all."

"Seriously?"

"The board, or Gerhard, apparently has decided my fate without discussing it with me."

"Well…. Congratulations."

"Thank you," I said through my teeth, looking over his shoulder to see reporters speaking to Cynthia, she pointed towards our direction.

"We need to leave."

I turned and started towards the elevators in the back of the building. James followed me, catching up and grabbing my arm.

"I'm not staying," I said, "You know how much I hate reporters."

James continued to pull, leading me off to the right. "Come on, you'll have to wait in line over at the elevators, we can lose them in the stairwell."

With the press conference just finishing up, the twin glass-lined elevators had a crowd forming, clogging Mendelium Tower's main artery. James led me towards a small hallway used by serving staff during events. We entered a stairwell and climbed.

"We don't have to go all the way up. A bit further and we can take the elevator from the third floor instead."

The first floor of Mendelium Tower was so tall that the second floor was nearly five stories off the ground. James went up the stairs two at a time in front of me and slid out the door. The lights dilated my eyes after exiting from the dark stairwell. We made our way through a break room on the far side past espresso machines and donuts. The elevator dinged in front of us. Sure enough, there was not a reporter in sight. A few people made their way off the elevator. We took up the spots left in the middle and turned to face the doors.

"Mornin' boys," Hayes said to us. The elevator attendant hit the button to the 87th floor without asking as soon as we walked into the elevator. He was sharply dressed, but he still had the look of someone who had grown up in the lower castes of society. I liked that about him, there were too many people in this building obsessed with climbing the corporate ladder.

"Good morning," I said, "How's your day been going?"

At times I wished I could have a job like his. Simple, with your mind free to wander at its unrestrained leisure. But these were only thoughts, the distraction of throwing myself into a problem and writing code was the one thing keeping me sane. The constant tics I would have if I was stuck in an elevator alone with my thoughts would drive me, and any other riders, completely mad.

"It's goin'. What are you fine gentlemen doing on the third floor? Taking a pit stop to steal a donut from the accountants? God knows they sure don't need 'em."

A few smiles flashed onto the faces of the group riding up with us. Familiar faces, but with thousands of Mendelium employees in the building this was the norm.

"We came up this way to dodge the reporters on the first floor—" I began, before James cut me off.

"Charlie here is the newest member of the board, and the press wants an interview."

"Congratulations," Hayes said, turning to give me a genuine smile.

"Thanks, Hayes."

The elevator stopped, and the display indicated we were on floor 57. A handful of the indistinct faces filtered off the elevator and a couple more entered. We rode up thirty more floors then James and I got off the lift. The Genetic Software and Engineering Department. Home sweet home.

"Good morning, James. Good morning, Charlie," said the receptionist as we passed through the entryway. Behind her the floor opened into a large area filled with desks; the entire east wall made of glass looking over the skyline. I made my way towards my office, walking around a couch area set up in the middle that coworkers used for project related conversation. I unlocked my door and sat down at my desk. The city was sunny and alive outside the window behind me. James strolled in behind me and shut the door.

"Well," he said, his casual demeanor fell away, "Why would they not talk to you first?"

I shrugged, "I was hoping you might have some ideas; the politics of this place isn't my game."

"How well does Gerhard know you?"

"He doesn't. I've had conversations with him here and there, but they have been brief. I think he and Dave were close, but I never was. Why?"

"Well normally Charlie, you don't go promoting someone to a board position without having a good idea of who they are as a person. Least of all you."

"Maybe Dave said good things about me?"

"Sure, because that sounds like something Dave would do," James said.

"Unless it directly benefited him, I can't imagine he would. The man does... did resent me, along with most of the board, Gerhard must have known that."

"Well, they voted you in," James said, "and after the speech you gave, I can't imagine why."

"Maybe there is a political reason behind it?" I said, "Gerhard is a little eccentric, getting more so every year. I swear he intentionally does things to piss people off sometimes."

"A 'little eccentric' is putting it lightly, have you ever been in his office? The place sticks out like a sore thumb from the rest of Mendelium Tower, it feels like a mixture of some old-time oil barons reading room and a meditation garden. Can you imagine how he even navigates through that thing in his wheelchair, I don't think…" James trailed off seeing me stand up out of my chair.

My entire life was changing with decisions completely outside my control. I couldn't just sit here and talk about it, I needed to know.

"That's a great idea James."

"What did I say?"

I walked past him and towards door.

"Where the hell are you going?" James said starting after me, narrowly missing one of the interns walking past.

"100th floor," I said back to him, "I'm going to get some answers."

CHAPTER 5

—

I t could have been the lack of sleep or the pounding
headache. It could have been my whole life shifting beneath my feet. I walked with an air of confidence that felt foreign to me. The elevator opened,
Hayes smiled, but my mind was already thirteen
stories above. A part of me expected to button to
the 100th floor to have an ominous hue, but Hayes'
finger pushed it, it lit up just like the rest, and we
began our ascent.

As the elevator stopped, the adrenaline of meeting
with one of the most powerful men in the world took
me out of my daze. Gerhard had an intimidating way
about him, his weathered, all-knowing face was plastered across so much of the city. His floor looked like
mine, but after a few strides the differences became
obvious. The bottom of the building was wider than
the top, my floor had offices in the center, with clus-
ters of people working and conversing across it. Here
at the peak, floor to ceiling windows reflected on all
sides, the cloudy skies felt as much a part of the room

as the polished slate floors. A receptionist sat directly ahead of me looking up with a cautious smile. I recognized the face but couldn't remember the name. He wore large dark rimmed glasses and a suit jacket that looked like it cost more money than my computer.

"Good morning, Charlie, how are you doing today?" he said, with a wide self-important smile. Walking up to his desk I saw a nameplate, Anthony Lin. His workspace was meticulously organized, the placement of his keyboard perfectly aligned with the pens that sat alongside it. The only item on his desk that didn't serve a function was a large yellow orchid sprouting from a white vase.

"Morning... Anthony," I said making no attempt to mirror his charm and excitement. "I need to speak with Gerhard."

"He is extremely busy, he's got back-to-back—"

"I know he's in the building. I imagine he'll be expecting me." I pointed to a small seating area off next to the full wall windows. "I'm going to take a seat and wait."

Anthony's smile fell, but he didn't object.

"Could you message him and let him know I am waiting? It would be appreciated." I flashed a half-hearted smile that did little to change his mood.

As I waited, the tightness in my chest faded and I eventually leaned into the seat. The angle of the waiting area allowed me to look down on one of Mendelium Tower's outcroppings. Jutting out on both sides, the two overlooks both held beautiful views of the city. They teemed with life—outdoor gardens hundreds of feet above the skyline.

"I understand," erupted Gerhard's voice from the elevator a few minutes later, "Now is not the time to discuss things... I've heard the same..."

Gerhard rolled past in his motorized chair. He wore a navy suit jacket, tailored perfectly to fit over his stump of an arm, his face was stern as he looked at me.

"It certainly does, thank you," he hung up the phone. "Mr. Lamarck."

"Morning Gerhard, we need to talk," I said looking down at him. The man that consumed and captivated rooms of people looked so small in front of me.

"I suppose we do."

"Sir, you have an appointment with the genetics ambassador from Belgium this morning, and afterwards a call with—" Anthony began, with a higher pitched voice than when he spoke to me.

"You are going to have to send Ruben my apologies and postpone, I have an urgent meeting with our newest board member."

Anthony pursed his lips together, giving me an empty smile with his too-white teeth, "Certainly sir, I'll let him know."

"Let's talk Charlie," Gerhard said, leading me towards the deep brown polished wooden doors of his office.

He pressed a button on his chair and the doors swung open in front of us. James was right, the space was so different than the rest of the building. Each wall of the long room had built-in bookshelves that looked a century old and refurbished. It felt more like a library than an office. Globes, plants, sculptures, and paintings with books on every inch between.

Gerhard rolled through the middle, dodging the couch the way one does when a place has the familiarity of home. In front of the couch was a fireplace. I did a double take—initially thinking it was fake—then realizing the man actually had a wood burning fireplace installed on the 100th floor of Mendelium Tower. *Was it necessary for all rich people to waste their money on things no person could ever need?* The lamps scattered throughout the shelves provided warm light to the room, but his desk against the far wall was lit by a floor to ceiling window overlooking the garden below, the city shimmering in the background. Gerhard rolled behind his desk, and I took a seat at one of the chairs directly across.

"How is your morning going?" he asked with a disarming smile.

"Not how I expected."

"No, I imagine not. I owe you an apology. It wasn't my intent for you to find out this way, the decision was made and I'm not a big believer in slow process and bureaucracy. The world—and you—had the right to know as soon as possible. You don't seem thrilled about the situation?"

I unfurled my brow and sat up straighter. "I'm honored, this is something most people would be thrilled to receive, but—"

"*Most* people?" Gerhard interjected with a surprised smile. "You don't?"

"Well… you heard my speech. The board, along with nearly everyone else at this company, has been distant since. I thought I was closer to being fired than I was to getting promoted."

My heart pounded in my chest, the momentum began, and the words flowed out of me like computer code.

"I'm frustrated with the direction of The Template. We are so quick to remove things from the human genome, something that might have value to society. I know it doesn't look like it, but I swear my condition has made me a better person and allowed me to have the level of success I've experienced. I might be wrong, but at the very least we can learn from people like me. We shape the future of mankind here, I could never have forgiven myself if I didn't speak my mind when given an opportunity."

I had barely spoken with this man; my entire career was in his palms if I upset him. *Was I too cavalier bursting into his office and forcing him to speak with me?*

His face remained stoic for a moment, then slowly, a smile formed, "You sure are chock-full of opinions Mr. Lamarck."

"So, I've been told."

"That speech—along with the one you gave a week ago—is exactly why you are here. I agree with you."

I leaned backward in my chair making no attempt to hide my surprise.

"Have you been in my office before?" he asked.

I shook my head.

"When I was a boy there were very few things I could enjoy with other kids. Having two mangled legs and a single functioning arm made it challenging to play with others. I lived a strange life; it was always hard for me to relate to other children.

"My parents ran a used bookstore out of our house. I grew up there, and not just figuratively, they couldn't afford both a store and a home, so they converted the entire first level into a bookstore and we lived upstairs. I took the elevator down in the morning, helped them out in ways I could, and in my down time I would read. To me books mean freedom. At first, they served as a way to escape. Then they became a way to refine my thinking—a tool to pursue the life I wanted.

"These shelves help me think," he said looking fondly around the room, "they remind me of where I've come from. They serve as a reminder of who I am, and never let me forget the knowledge my parents shared with me. They also remind me that without the misfortunes I was born with I never would have read the books and learned the lessons I have. I never would have become obsessed with finding out about genetics, or why I am the way I am. I never would have started Mendelium.

"You spoke to me more than you know. You are not the only one that thinks this way, and you are not the only one who feels ignored. I have a proposition for you Charlie, one I hope you will consider."

CHAPTER 6

THREE YEARS EARLIER

The smell of coffee beans filled the entryway of the cafe, it was a much-needed reprieve from my desk. It was large for a coffee shop in the heart of the city, with multiple baristas and a long line of customers snaking through the place.

I needed some caffeine to push through the pains of my new position. I used to have so much control over my days and who I worked with, but that time was gone. Each week dragged by, I regretted my decision to sell to Mendelium every day over the last three months.

Coffee used to be one of the small moments I looked forward to in the day. The casual conversations with my coworkers and employees, they were the people I worked for, the ones who gave my life meaning.

That phase of my life was over.

The warmth of my old coffee breaks replaced by the cold corporate routine of paying for my coffee at a location far away from my desk. At least it wasn't some big chain, the unique designs and the locally roasted beans were a small win. I may have sold out and messed up the largest decision of my entire life, but this tiny decision I was determined to get right.

Today the line barely moved, the anxiousness visible in the patrons. Some checked the clock on the wall, some buried their face in a phone. I just took in the smells of the coffee beans. Two ladies stood in front of me, one of them wore a tank top, and I noticed a Template device attached to her arm. They were snickering, joking about a woman up near the front of the store. Next to the pastries, there were racks of coffee beans lining a tall wooden shelf, she knelt next to them, sorting through each. I'd never purchased any beans, preferring the convenience of someone else preparing my coffee. The wall was lined with brightly colored bags of varying sizes. The woman didn't look like she had any intent on purchasing one.

The two ladies in front of me continued, "What do you think is *wrong* with her? How little must you have going on in your life to start organizing a shelf at a random coffee shop."

I was grateful to be standing behind them. It was typically me that endured the whispers and rude remarks, it felt strange to be a background character rather than the focal point of the mocking. The woman knelt on the ground, grabbing bags on the shelf, and sorting them in order of size. I didn't laugh. I'd lived on the other side of those laughs for too many years, she looked frustrated and exhausted. A woman like *that* wouldn't call me crazy. A woman like *that* won't make me feel like some freak while I sit across the table from her. With my head buried in a computer for much of the day I've always considered myself oblivious to some of the more human urges people feel. This one I couldn't ignore.

I wasn't sure what I was doing, breaking from the line of waiting people. I wasn't sure what I would say when I got over to her, so I knelt next to her and smiled. Her braided blond hair swaying as she moved between bags, as soon as she saw me, she looked taken aback. I didn't speak, I just grabbed a bag and began following the same sorting order she'd been using. With a bemused look on her face the two of us continued for a few minutes before wrapping up the job.

"I'm Elizabeth," she said, brushing off her hands and glancing at the crowd of people who were now shooting both of us strange looks.

"Charlie," I said, "Could I buy your drink? If you still have to pay. This coffee shop should be giving you one on the house for all the free labor you just gave them."

She gave a quick snort of a laugh. "My life has been spiraling out of control lately. I knocked over a single bag, I put it back then straightened out an entire row—I don't think I realized what was happening until I'd nearly finished. With everything else in my life so confusing it felt good to organize something... I promise you, I'm not usually this crazy."

"I was kind of hoping that you were," I said back.

She looked at me curiously, but her face slowly turned into a smile. I stood up offering a hand to help her to her feet. She took it, and I pulled her up close to me for a moment. A hint of her floral perfume cut through the coffee beans, she stood nearly as tall as me, her round eyes lingering on mine.

"Yes," she said.

"Yes, to what?"

"To the coffee."

I blinked, astonished by her interest in the offer. I was so caught up in the moment my thinking mind barely had time to analyze my words. I was surprised this beautiful woman had just said yes to me, but more so that I'd even asked her in the first place. These last few months felt like I was sleepwalking, her soft smiling face jolted me awake.

The long rush hour line was now short, the two ladies who'd joked about her mixed into the crowds passing through the city. The two of us stepped up and both ordered our drinks, then found a quiet corner to ourselves.

"So, what do you do Elizabeth? When you aren't moonlighting as a barista."

"As of 9:30 this morning, nothing, my boss just fired me."

"I'm so sorry," I said, still surprised that this beautiful woman was sitting across from me sipping on a latte.

"Don't be, she was a terrible person. I put my heart into my work, constantly going above and beyond, so she fired me."

The curious look on my face must have prompted her to continue.

"I worked at an event planning firm, the largest in town. I'd been there for a while and loved everything about the job... everything except her. I enjoyed the work, the balancing of so many things happening at once, being able to share the big moments of our clients lives. It brought me joy, but I completely ignored the office politics. Apparently, there were whispers of moving me into her position."

"So, she fired you? For being too good at your job?"

She just smiled back at me. People moved past the windows outside the coffee shop, and the commotions continued as the baristas made customers drinks, but that fell to the background as I watched her tell her story.

"I don't know what I'm going to do now. I cared for my clients so much. All those relationships I'd built, I won't be able to work with those people anymore. My life feels like it's spiraling out of control," she wiped one of the tears welling up in her eyes. "I'm so sorry, today has been terrible. You don't want to hear any of this. What is it you do, Charlie? When you're not helping crazy women organize shelves at a coffee shop."

"Well sometimes I go to grocery stores and help strange women organize cereal boxes."

She laughed, the sadness on her face completely gone for a moment. I paused, enjoying seeing the way her face carried a smile.

"I just don't know what I'm going to do next," she said. "I made promises to so many of those people, newlyweds planning their weddings and a ninety-year-old's surprise birthday party I've been more excited for than anything. All those relationships I built are gone. What's worse is that I know she won't do nearly as good a job as I would have. Those people entrusted me, and now I've let them down."

"But it wasn't your fault," I said.

"It feels that way."

"Is there any way you could still help them?" I asked.

"What do you mean?"

"Did you sign any contract saying you wouldn't compete with them?"

"Never."

"It sounds to me like you care about these people a lot more than your firm does. What if you started your own event planning firm? You could reach out to all those people. I can see how much you care about them, I'm sure some would be happy to work with you instead."

"There is no way I could do something like that. I have no experience in business, I just want to help people plan their events, I'll have to find some other company to work for. I can't just start my own firm in this city, I have no idea where to begin."

"That's what I said too, before I started mine."

She looked at me, I held her gaze. There was something I couldn't place about her, something in the way she held herself. I felt lighter and my heartbeat quickened, I hadn't even taken a sip my coffee yet.

"You never did tell me what it was you did," she said.

"I work at Mendelium," I said, "before that I ran a small company. The only thing I thought I ever wanted to do was write code and build things, but I found out along the way that it is deeply rewarding being on a team and helping other people."

"I couldn't agree more," she said, leaning closer to me.

"I messed up badly, Elizabeth. I lost sight of what mattered the most and I sold the company to

Mendelium, I let all those people down and I regret it every day. If I had an opportunity to do something more, or to help the people that matter to me, I would go for it. I've known you for all of ten minutes, so feel free to ignore my opinions, but I can see the way you care about people. I can see your love for them in the way you speak, it would be a travesty to ignore that."

She looked back at me, golden hair hanging over the side of her shoulder. I wanted to freeze in this moment, to take a mental picture of this dazzling woman with a curious smile.

"What are you doing for dinner tomorrow night?" I asked, the words tumbling out before I even realized I was saying them.

"Nothing at all."

"I would like... do you... want to go to dinner with me?" I asked.

"I'd love to."

CHAPTER 7

——

Liz and I sped down the road, the sun slowly sinking in the rearview mirror. The car drove itself, swallowing up the yellow lines beneath its steel belly, using artificial intelligence and mountains of data to ensure our safety. As an engineer I couldn't help but marvel at the technology. I imagined the millions of lines of computer code that allowed this car to weave through the traffic.

One hundred years ago people thought flying cars would be traversing the planet by now, yet here we were still navigating down the same weathered interstates. It reminded me of the Template. People envisioned genetic manipulation would create humans with different color hair or designer traits, but that was so far from the reality.

Why build a flying car when we already had a preexisting road infrastructure in place? That's how humanity progresses, we iterate on the old technologies. Massive cities like Paris were built on top of ancient sewer systems. Self-driving cars still rattled down poorly kept roadways because it was an easier way to solve that problem then it was to create an entirely different machine. Why deal with the engineering challenges of flying around in three dimensions when roads already existed, and webs of interconnected vehicles could move around through cities in perfect unison.

The same was true of Mendelium. Technically we could grow a child in a test tube, but why not leverage humanities preexisting infrastructure? In this case the mother's womb. Instead of manipulating humans from scratch we simply modify the mothers blood stream, ensuring the proper nutrient and chemical levels to guarantee specific traits in the child. Nature did it better than we ever could, Gerhard's brilliance was ditching the test tubes and embracing what already existed.

"Just he and his daughter?" Liz asked me, shocking me back to the realities of the present moment.

"I think so, but he's a strange guy," I said. "He didn't tell me much besides his address and what time to be there."

"I'm curious to see how they live," she said, staring out her passenger window, we passed by more trees driving further from the city. She wore a navy blazer, contrasting her golden hair. The sort of thing that to me seemed like an accident, but I imagine she meticulously decided. I wore jeans and the sweater she'd recommended.

"It's bound to be unique," I said, adjusting my collar for the fourth time in the last minute. *Just what I needed before an important dinner, a new tic.* "If it's anything like his office it will look like an old library."

"Library?" she asked, turning her gaze from the passing landscape over to me.

"He's got a thing for books; says they help him think."

"Interesting, you don't see too many physical copies these days. What about his daughter?"

"Grace."

"Just the two of them?" She asked, with a hint of sadness in her face.

"I'm sure he has some staff around, but yes," I said, the car exiting off of the interstate and onto one of the smaller roads running out into the woods. I straightened my collar again, the repetitiveness of the task slipping into a feeling of reflex, the tic no longer conscious.

"How long ago did his wife pass?" she asked.

"Two years. Are you planning on using all of this in the conversation or something?"

"I'm being prepared," she said looking at me proudly. "It's a part of my profession, I've got to keep my socializing and knowing-things skills sharp. I have to make up for how terrible you are at small talk."

"I'm great at big talk."

She rolled her eyes. We were officially outside the city, patches of trees outnumbered houses. I was happy he'd invited Liz and I both to dinner, I was curious about his proposal, but I wasn't as socially perceptive as Liz. I looked forward to having her there to cross examine Gerhard.

"Does he seem like a good father?" She asked, leaning her head back into the seat. These sorts of questions were becoming more frequent with each passing month. I still wasn't sure how to navigate them. We'd spoken so much of having children, but these were feeling less like hypothetical conversations. I ticced again, grabbing onto my shirt collar. Could I really be a good father to a child? Fatherhood always seemed like something that people saner than me did. I had hoped that more time would make me feel capable, but it was only serving to do the opposite. If anything, I now felt more alienated from the rest of the world, my thoughts and opinions were so different from everyone at Mendelium, was different really what a child needed in a father?

"He's been withdrawn since his wife Carmen died. I imagine he's been dedicating more of his time to Grace."

The car turned again, this road even smaller than the last.

"Would you ever like to live this far outside of the city?" she asked.

"We both live so close to work," I said, as the car slowed, rounding a corner. "And I think the cost would be prohibitive."

"Outside of the logical reasons Charlie, would you like it out here?" she asked, pulling down the mirror and checking her appearance again.

"I can't separate those two things. Being financially viable means less stress, being closer to work means less commute and the time gained each day compounds over time."

"What about raising a family?" She asked, sitting back from the mirror looking satisfied with her appearance.

"Access to the outdoors would be good for children, but I hate commuting. When we have kids, we are going to need to be as efficient as possible if we want any chance of continuing our careers."

She turned back away looking out the window and chewing on her lip. The forest made everything seem darker, and the foreign road winding more than I was used to didn't help. We turned down another road, still paved, but houses no longer lined the road. I noticed Liz sit upright in her seat, it continued getting more secluded. The road stopped, ahead of us a large stone archway with a gate at the far end covered the road.

"Well, this is bound to be it," I said as the car passed through the archway. To my left was a window and a round smiling face right behind it.

"Welcome Charlie. Welcome Elizabeth," said an old man, his voice coming through the gap in the glass below his face. His voice cracked, the deep lines in his face shadowed by the single light hanging above. "Gerhard and Grace are expecting you," he said, gesturing for us to move along.

The metal gate slowly expanded. We continued down a road until the trees opened in front of us. A dark lawn loomed to our left side; a small rock wall held back the scraggly trees from overtaking the grounds. Liz stared out her window over a large lake on the opposite, touches of light glimmered across reflecting on the property in front of us. I ticced, straightening my collar two more times.

"Wow," Liz said staring across the lake. A few tiny houses peppered the far side off in the distance.

"I didn't know this lake existed so close to the city," Liz said sitting up in her seat.

The mansion had walls of stone, but it was clear the construction wasn't as old as the rocks tried to make it seem. Three stories tall with multiple castle-like spires on the side of the house facing the lake, large glass windows on all sides.

Of course, Gerhard would make his home look like a castle.

My stomach turned, I felt out of my depth. I walked behind the car and opened Liz's door. My mind raced about dinner etiquette and what Gerhard was expecting of us. This place had surely seen some wealthy dinner parties well above anything we had attended. I took Liz's arm as we walked up the multiple ramps and past immaculately manicured flowers. Before my finger could press the doorbell, the large wooden front door flung open in front of us.

"Welcome," Gerhard announced, sitting in front of us in an old-school metal wheelchair. There were stains on his worn apron, the sleeve of his good arm rolled up. The large welcoming smile seemed so out of place on the distinguished face.

"Come in, come in," he gestured and backed up to let us step inside the house. "Thank you both so much for making it out here, we're excited to have you."

"It's our pleasure," I said, returning the smile, grateful for his relaxed appearance.

"You have a beautiful home," Liz said while taking off her coat, "the lake and grounds are stunning."

"Thank you, this is where a better dinner host would take your coat for you, but that sort of thing isn't my forte," he said, raising up his stub of a left arm. "Did you appreciate our entry ramp?"

"It… was nice," I said, confused.

"I enjoy making you spoiled bipedal people feel my pain. I have a complicated relationship with stairs, it seems like everywhere I go they are silently reminding me of my inadequacies. There is no other way into this place, a slow entry ramp for everyone. My contractors argued—but I stand by the decision."

Liz chuckled while the two of us followed Gerhard through to the kitchen. The decoration contrasted with his office at Mendelium Tower, the walls were white, cover with warm artwork. Soft orange rays from the setting sun painting the walls. We followed as Gerhard led us through a dining room and past a table that could have sat twenty people. The sound of jingling pans came from the kitchen.

"I would like you to meet my Sous-chef," Gerhard said as we entered the kitchen, "the lovely and talented Grace Geller."

A small head of brown hair bobbed up and down closing pantry doors and putting away pans. She poked her head up over the counter and gave us a forced smile and a wave and went back to putting away dishes.

"We take cooking seriously in this household," Gerhard said. "It's become our new hobby. How are the carrots doing, Grace?" Gerhard asked.

"Three minutes and 46 seconds," she said, spinning towards her dish and stirring. "The potatoes have 7 minutes and 22 seconds."

"We are also extremely specific," Gerhard said to us with a smile. "Can you come and introduce yourself to the Lamarcks?"

"I'm Grace," she said cautiously leaving the kitchen, looking at her feet while she spoke, "who are you?"

"I'm Charlie," I responded attempting a welcoming smile. "This is Elizabeth."

"Hi Grace," Liz said, voice higher pitched than normal. "You sure look like you know what you are doing in the kitchen."

"Ya, I'm a pretty good cook," she said looking over her shoulder to a simmering pan on the stove, "my best dish is pasta, but Dad wanted to try something different tonight."

"You've got Pasta alla Norma down, I wanted to give you some new challenges," Gerhard said as she turned back to the kitchen. "And eating it for the last seventeen nights has been getting a bit boring" he whispered behind the back of his hand.

It was humanizing to see Gerhard in such a casual situation with his daughter, the intimidation that I normally felt in his presence mellowed. The kitchen was alive with smells, water boiled on the stove and a candle flickered on the small dinner table to the side of the kitchen.

"What are you making for us today, Grace?" Liz asked while Grace stirred one of the dishes on the stove.

"Beef tenderloin with shallots," she reported, "steamed carrots and potatoes on the side"

"Well, that sounds delicious," Liz said. "Have you made this before?"

"Never," she responded, "but Dad says we have to try new things if we want to become better cooks."

"Wise man," I said. "How long have you been cooking? You look like you could give me a few tips?"

Grace finished pulling the carrots off the stove and took a look in the oven, then walked over, and puffed out her chest proudly.

"My mom was a great cook, but I've gotten pretty good," she said.

"So, you like to make Italian dishes the best, what are some of your other favorites?" Liz asked.

"Well, desert obviously. But I'm not very good at baking, oh, and I really like to make breakfast food."

Liz looked over and smiled at me. It hurt me to see how much she lit up around children when we still didn't have any of our own. A part of me was still intimidated by children, seeing Liz function so smoothly with them made me less confident I would have the right disposition to be a father.

"Breakfast is my favorite too," I said. "How do you like your eggs?"

Her eyes lit up again, "Scrambled, for sure. But I'm really good at making poached eggs as well, do you want to see?"

"And what do you imagine poached eggs would go with in our meal, Grace?" Gerhard asked, now rolling around the dinner table with settings for four.

"I don't care what your dad says, I'd take a poached egg on the side," I joked looking between both Gerhard and Grace. He smiled at me and spoke again, "I'm sure the Lamarcks are plenty impressed by all of the hats you are wearing right now."

Grace looked confused, she put her hand on her hair patting a couple of times, "I'm not wearing a hat at all, Dad"

"It's an expression, sweetheart," Gerhard smiled.

"Your dad is right," Liz said looking at Gerhard, "I'm impressed, I still end up burning things when trying to manage a few dishes at once."

Grace blushed and moved back in front of the stove, stepping on her stool again putting dishes into the sink. Liz and I continued to look on as she grabbed the different pans off the stove and began to plate the different pieces of the meal. She hopped across the kitchen moving from one side to the other with an intense focus. It didn't take long before all four plates had been put together and sat at the table to eat.

"This looks fantastic," Liz commented while Gerhard brought the last of the drinks and utensils over to the center of the table.

I smiled and watched, still fascinated by the relationship between her and Gerhard and seeing him in this new environment. She smiled at Liz and thanked her.

Then we ate. Grace explaining the details of her favorite dishes, Liz and I enjoyed seeing how passionate she was about cooking. The conversation bounced in many directions; in the way they do with an eight-year-old as a dinner guest.

With every bite I grew more fascinated with Grace, her cooking skills were so impressive for a child so young. But more than that, her obsession with the topic was peculiar. The strangeness continued throughout the dinner with Gerhard. He seemed thrilled to watch his daughter speaking enthusiastically with us, but beyond flashes of a smile was something else in his eyes, something subtle, something filled with pain.

CHAPTER 8

———

"They sure are enjoying themselves," Gerhard said, as the two of us looked back at Liz and Grace. Gerhard clicked a button to open the door outside and gestured for me to lead.

"This isn't the night I was expecting," I said as I walked out into the crisp fall air. "We'd been stressing about attending a formal dinner, but this was perfect."

"I'm glad," he said rolling down the switchback ramps on the back of his house. "I don't have much experience on the matter, but I've been told walking does the brain good."

I chuckled, "You've been told right."

"Good, I want your brain working full well," Gerhard said. We moved onto a concrete path descending into the woods and towards the lake, the forest was dark, but lights lined the entire path, the sun's final rays flickering over the water.

"So, what's this proposition?" I asked.

"We'll get there," Gerhard said, "but first I have a question. Before being purchased by Mendelium you took GeniSense from a small startup to over one hundred people. That's not an easy feat. Running one of the largest companies in the world is a difficult task. But as difficult as things are now, the early days were the most challenging. You accomplished something truly impressive."

"And then we were purchased to improve Mendelium's supply chain."

"Don't sell yourself short Charlie. I've talked to the people you used to work with, GeniSense succeeded because of your work ethic and talent."

I nodded, "Still not a question."

"Do you think you would have been able to do that without having Tourette's syndrome?"

I paused for a moment, taken aback by the question. *What had I expected?* He said he wanted to talk about my speech, I had shared so much about myself with the world. He knew something about me that I used to keep shielded, it felt strange to hear the words from another human, especially from one of the most powerful men in the world. "No, I don't believe I would."

"I had a hunch," he said, still rolling down the path.

"I owe so much of my life to it," I said. "Focusing on code used to be my way to cope. I don't know where life might have taken me if I didn't find programming when I did. The deep flow states of writing code with just my brain and the problem were my only escape, whether from the tics or... other events in my life. It helped me forget about the pain of my physical body."

"I feel similarly," he said, "our life situations shape who we become. In both of our cases our negative situations made the world—and those around us—better. As Mendelium has seen success, I've had the opportunity to interact with many fascinating people. Individuals that change the world with every decision, nearly all of them went through difficult things in their youth.

"This pattern continues across great thinkers from the past. Stephen Hawking would never have discovered black holes if not for the urgency of his impending death from ALS. Vincent van Gogh was plagued by psychiatric illness his entire life, but out of his tortured mind came a beautiful new way to look at the world. Teddy Roosevelt had severe bronchial asthma as a child. The illness inspired a love for the outdoors, leading him to conserve over 100 million acres of land during his presidency."

The lights flashed by one at a time, the rhythm of walking and the smell of the breeze off the lake supplied a backdrop to our conversation.

"Hard times make hard people. Most of us instinctively understand this truth, but not many today have lived it. For you and me this lesson is more concrete, it has defined our lives. The same fire that lives in my soul burns in yours."

I nodded reflexively. *This long preamble, the dinner and wine, what is it you want?*

"We sprint towards comfort as a society, only to realize comfort doesn't equate to happiness. You and I have learned this lesson in the one way I believe a person can, through experience. I want you to understand where I am coming from, I want you to know how much your words resonated with me on the day of your speech."

"It is a relief to hear someone on the board agrees with me... but you head a company founded on optimizing the human genome."

We slowed to a stop and the forest opened to reveal the lake. A dock extended into the gentle waves. I followed Gerhard to the end of it. In the darkness I was able to see the small lights of houses across the lake, a couple stars beginning to spatter the sky.

"Our understanding of genetics and evolution is in its infancy," he began. "The things we do here at Mendelium are brilliant, but it wouldn't be the first time that innovative science brought carnage to the world. We are making irreversible decisions about the future of humanity. Decisions rooted in fear. No parent wants their child at a disadvantage, no one wants a crippled son or a depressed daughter if given the choice. Our culture's fear of these outcomes is driving us to eradicate genes from existence, but we still barely understand why these traits come about in the first place.

"Life is a beautiful thing; evolutionary systems have worked infallibly for years. I don't think we've begun to understand how much risk we are taking in trying to manipulate this process. I invited you over tonight to help rectify that.

"I've made a mistake. One that's snowballed over time, I can no longer sit idly watching the work we do. Our teams toil over what genes to remove from existence, but what if the entire framework we base this around is wrong?"

The waves lapped against the shore while we sat there in momentary silence.

"What is it that you want from me, Gerhard?"

"I want to help you, Charlie, and I want you to understand why. You made your argument for keeping Tourette's syndrome in the gene pool, I want to help make that happen."

I looked around at the grounds, down to the light of his house that glimmered against the dancing waves. "All of this, everything you have is because of the Template."

"That's exactly why this is so urgent," he said. "It eats me alive knowing the beautiful life I've created here for Grace—my entire life's accomplishments— are misaligned with my beliefs. It started pure. We found a way to guarantee no child would ever face the life I experienced. I thought it was what was best for the world at the time, but now our problems are gone, and the tools still exist. We look at every imperfection like it's a disease. Patching up the bugs of evolution, trying to outsmart life itself. It's this trend that scares me, it's not the legacy I want to leave on the world."

"What exactly are you proposing?"

He took his gaze off the homes lining the opposite shores of the lake and directed it straight to me, turning his chair square in my direction. "You sold me, Charlie."

"On what exactly?"

"On you. On Tourette's syndrome. We shouldn't remove it in this year's Template."

"But it's already been done, the board voted. *You* voted."

"That brings me to my proposal," he said, his piercing green eyes reflecting the lights from the dock. "Things may be in motion, but they are far from finished. There is still time to change it, but I need your help."

CHAPTER 9

TWO AND A HALF
YEARS EARLIER

"You know I'm not new anymore," I said as James walked into the room, moving slower than usual. "You don't need to keep hanging out with me."

"As a member of Mendelium's human resources department I'm contractually obligated to make sure you are comfortable here," he said with a wink. He rifled through his bag and winced in pain as he sat at one of the couches next to me. I liked this secluded corner of the office. If I was at my desk people could come in to ask me questions and distract me. The location never mattered; my home was wherever my computer was. Down here I could be alone with the code—with the occasional welcomed distraction from James.

"Pretty sure I've been 'comfortable here' for months," I air quoted. "Can't you see me working and satisfied?"

He let out an exaggerated sigh as he slowly lowered himself further into the chair across from me. "What happened to me? I used to be able to train with the best of them, now if I sleep wrong, I'm sore the entire next day."

He clasped at his back massaging one of his muscles there, his face in pain.

"You got old," I said.

"I suppose," he said sitting back, grimacing. "You should have seen me back in the day, I could fly across hurdles, even throw a javelin."

"I don't know why you're telling me," I said, taking my eyes off the screen to look at him. Pulling my brain out of the code and into reality. "Athletics weren't exactly my forte."

"No," he began, "I suppose not. But do you really think that your brain functions as well as it used to when you were younger?"

I smiled and nodded, "For the most part. Maybe I'm a little less neurotic now. As long as I have a problem to throw myself at time fades away and I can focus on anything for as long as I want."

"I think you'd be surprised how rare that is."

"I've realized that. Most people need a caffeine fix to drag them through the morning, I love the taste of coffee, but I don't need the caffeine if the work is interesting. It seems like everyone else needs it to hit their deadlines."

"Or something stronger," James said, looking at me sternly.

"What's that supposed to mean?"

"Caffeine is a strange drug," he said. "Most central nervous system stimulants aren't readily available and encouraged by your employer. Everyone turns a blind eye to the brown liquid that two thirds of the population is physically addicted to."

I didn't say anything back to him. It was such an odd way to look at a harmless pleasure people enjoy every day.

"You know that you have a calmness about you I've seen in very few people, Charlie."

"It certainly doesn't feel that way."

"You spend your days doing what you love, and you are damn good at it. I'm envious of that, you know?"

"You seem pretty content being able to talk with people most of the day. Meeting new faces and making connections. You can't tell me you don't enjoy some element of that?"

James shifted a little in his seat, still looking slightly uncomfortable, "I do. But there is something else too, nearly everyone else around here seems like they are striving for something more. Racing to compete with one another, fighting for every advantage they can grab onto. I've never seen any of that in you."

"Thanks," I said, not quite sure what to think about the direction of our conversation. "I'm always trying to solve problems, to fix my small corner of the world. Maybe that prevents me from worrying about the big things?"

"Maybe," he said, still looking at me funny. "You know I think that might be why I like you so much C, you might be the only person in this whole building who doesn't need what I have to offer."

"And what exactly is that?"

"Quite a few different things actually. Can I be open with you about something?"

"Of course."

"Human Resources isn't my only source of income. I have a side hustle—a rather successful one."

"How do you even have time? I feel like you spend as much time networking as anyone."

"Well, you see, I'm actually working right now. In a few moments a young woman is going to walk through that door and I'm going to sell her some drugs."

"What?" I said. He had a smile on his face, one that I didn't know how to read into.

"I deal," he continued. "Always have. During college, the athletic scholarships I received were the only way I was able to afford my education. I had to perform at a high-level day after day. I was forced to perform athletically to retain my scholarship and academically if I wanted to graduate. I was determined to find a way to make things easier on myself, it wasn't particularly difficult. Acquiring the right substances was easier than I expected but learning how to use them was what was the most challenging. I learned more studying how to optimize my body and mind than I did in my degree."

"Did that actually work?" I asked, still not sure how I should be responding to all of this. *What did he want from me?* I tried to keep any judgment out of my eyes, he was opening up to me, no matter what he said I simply needed to listen.

"Hugely," he said. "It completely transformed my performance; I was able to operate at a higher level ensuring I was able to keep my scholarship and stay in school. It started as a small advantage, but the more I learned and the more I experimented the better I got—eventually, people noticed."

"Did you ever feel morally conflicted about it? It's sort of like cheating in a sense, isn't it?"

"Absolutely," he said, "I'll never claim what I was doing was fair, but there is something you must understand. As a student athlete, in order to keep getting my scholarships there was a certain level of physical and mental performance I had to keep up with. It wasn't just about competing anymore, my entire life depended on my performance, all my team's lives did. What could I do but share my wisdom? Learning how to use performance enhancers improved my life so much, it seemed like something I should share with those around me. It started out as me simply helping them, I never expected for it to turn into such a profitable business.

"Want to get stronger? There is a drug for that. Need to recover better? I know exactly which type of pill and dosing strategy you need. Did you struggle focusing on your studies? Well, I had just the thing to fix it. It didn't take long before I was an expert at enhancing my team's performance. The pole-vaulters, the distance runners, the shot put and discus throwers—everyone had their own unique challenges. Before long I was having more fun helping them find ways to improve than I did in school.

"The coaches during my time liked to think our track and field team flourished because of their perfect management. Little did they know most of their student athletes were taking performance enhancers of one kind or another."

I just stared back at him, slowly nodding, hoping to encourage him to tell me more. His appearance seemed to change as the words spilled out of him, they painted in some backstory of his I didn't know before. Slowly the picture of James crystalized.

"It stuck with me," he continued, "once you begin chasing performance it's hard to stop. I was operating at the highest levels athletically and academically, and I was making enough money on the side to fund my education. College ended, and a part of me thought that I would simply stop, life would become easier then and I would slow down. The opposite happened. I got an internship at Mendelium and realized the cycle had begun anew. There were a new set of challenges, a new set of criteria to optimize for. On top of that, there was an entirely new clientele. No longer would I have to cater to the poor college athletes of the world, now I worked side-by-side with wealthy high achievers at one of the fastest growing companies in the world.

"I love my job; the Human Resources department allows me to meet most of the incredible people that come through here. But what I really love is helping people to perform at their highest levels."

"Why are you telling me this?" I asked.

"It's been eating at me," he said. "You have one of the most unique views on work of anyone I've met here. Most people are interested in drugs to help them perform better at work. For you, work *is the drug*, there is nothing I can offer you that you don't already have. Usually, I ask imploring questions as I meet people, it was clear from day one you weren't interested. You might be the only person in this whole building who has no interest in being a client of mine."

"I'm still not," I said.

"I'm not telling you because I thought you were. I'm telling you because I like you Charlie—I want you to know what I do, and why I do it. I know this is a lot, but it already feels so much better to get it off my chest. Do you think you can be comfortable with this?"

How many of my coworkers knew about this side of James? Not only had he opened up to me, but my entire view of Mendelium felt like it shifted, a dirty secret completely hidden from my own view. This world was foreign to me, but was it *wrong*? If anything, I was the strange one, able to focus for insane hours at a time and letting the world slip away. Was it really so bad that others desired the same abilities that I came by naturally?

"I suppose it's not much different from me drinking coffee to wake up in the morning," I said, still trying to form an opinion about his side gig.

"Exactly," he said. He stood up, clenching at his back again. A young brunette woman I recognized from one of the research departments entered the room, flashing a knowing smile at James. "If you'll excuse me Charlie, I have some business to attend to."

CHAPTER 10

———

Normally I would be hungover after an evening of wine, but something was alive inside me that lay dormant before. I expected to wake up feeling regretful of my conversation with Gerhard, but things felt right. I could feel it in the way I carried myself to work in the morning, and in the way I kissed Liz as she left for work. The mundane routines, the commute, and small talk all seemed more vibrant—the colors saturated.

The two of us shared some deep-seated beliefs, and we might even be able to do something about them. These thoughts carried me through the day. Maybe I could rework the talk I had already given at Mendelium, with Gerhard's buy-in we could get a new message out to the world? There still might be hope for Tourette's syndrome.

I sat in my office, door open, sounds of the floor seeping in. The responsibilities of being on the board becoming apparent, work was taking up more of my time. The sun dipped towards the horizon, the haze of the sky taking on a soft orange glow. Footsteps approached my door, I pulled myself out of my head.

"Hey C," James said, rounding the corner and sliding into my office. "How's the day going?"

I smiled at him as he walked in to take a seat across from me. "I'm realizing why Dave was such an ass. There is simply too much work crammed into one day. I don't have any time to think."

"I don't buy that for a second, you and Dave couldn't be more different people if you tried."

"I do try," I said, "I spend time every day thinking about what Dave might have done and then do the opposite."

James chuckled.

"Can I ask you something?" I asked abruptly, switching to a serious tone faster than I intended. "What do you think will come of the Template in the future?"

"What do you mean?" he asked, lounging back in the chair.

"How do you think it will evolve? This whole process is in its infancy, we have taken care of the obvious positive changes, and now it seems parents are fighting for smaller and smaller optimizations."

"Is this what they pay you to think about now that you're on the board and have this new fancy office?"

"Over the last ten years the Template has been refined rapidly, there aren't as many obvious optimizations as there once were. But parents continue demanding changes, what do you think the Template will look like in another decade?"

"It'll continue I suppose," he said, taking his time to respond. "We will keep finding optimizations, new things that will make future generations better."

"Sure," I replied, "But we've already eliminated most of the low hanging fruit, then what?"

"More recently we have upped markers for intelligence, decreased likelihood of Alzheimer's and dementia."

I nodded along, "Excellent examples, but what has driven these changes?"

He paused and thought for a moment again, a trait of his I appreciated. So many people at Mendelium flung words around recklessly, saying anything to sound intelligent. James took the time to give me an honest response.

"Parents," he said.

"Exactly," I said, "specifically their money."

"The beauty of free market economics," he winked.

"Are there any downsides to this system?" I asked him again.

"Well…" he started and looked at me curiously, "Societally we are going to keep optimizing, it's what we humans do. Right now, our system incentivizes health and happiness."

"Do you see any problems with that?" I asked.

"Nothing… well, nothing obvious. I have a hard time believing that making a happier and healthier society is such a bad thing."

"It's subtle," I said nodding again. "It's similar to investing in a lot of ways. You own a fair amount of Mendelium stock, right?"

He nodded.

"Do you own other investments?"

"Sure," he said. He was always short with me when discussing financials. He had some income streams he wasn't particularly fond of talking about in the office.

"Good looking *and* smart with his money," I said with a smile, "Since you are an intelligent investor, you follow the principle of diversification. Having other investments helps to reduce risk, ensuring in bad times you can weather the storm. If Mendelium fails, the rest of your investments keep you from losing everything.

"By refining the Template down further we reduce genetic diversification. This makes sense on an individual level. It is only normal for a parent to want the best for their child. But two things are happening in tandem. First, Template usage is at an all-time high. It's not just the rich elite paying for an advantage for their children anymore, most people use the product. Second, we continue to refine the Template. Humanity now has less genetic diversity than ever before, and it's *decreasing* exponentially."

James nodded along with me the entire time. "Sure," he said, "but how high is the risk, Charlie? What are the dangers?"

"That's just it," I said, "We have no idea. No other species has manipulated their genome in the way we are now capable of. We are doing so rapidly, with no way to look at the long-term repercussions."

"What *could* we do about it?" He asked.

I shrugged, "The trends of refining are going to continue, that seems like a certainty. Template usage has grown every year for the last decade."

"Parents aren't likely to start endowing their children with worse genes," James said.

"No, they are not," I agreed.

"Where does that leave us?" He asked, tone more serious than before.

"Do you think we could educate society on the issue?" I asked, "If we did, do you think anything would stop?"

"Older people have always been slow to adopt new technologies," he stated. "They kick and scream until they eventually give up the fight and let it happen. Maybe this is just our generation's version of that? We may not agree with this direction, but it's something outside of our control, what good is it to worry? If you keep talking like this someone might lump you in with those crazy anti-Template protesters standing out front. Might as well focus on you and me, right here and right now."

I smiled at him. Talking with James typically calmed my nerves, but in this case, it did the opposite. This wasn't something outside of my control any longer, I had the responsibility to do *something,* and I might even have some buy-in from the most powerful man in genetics.

"You know what Charlie? All this speculating is making me hungry, do you want to grab some dinner and get out of here a little bit early? Some people are going for drinks, it could do you some good to take your mind off work for a little while."

I breathed out, trying to push the weight bearing down on my chest out through my lungs. "I could use a distraction."

I flicked off the light in my office and the two of us left the room. I looked back at it as we walked across the floor and through the communal area, it still didn't feel completely real, the room was mine now, but I still felt like the same man I was before. My confidence had continued to grow since taking on the board position, but no matter what I changed about myself I still felt the pangs of self-doubt.

Was I capable of making real change?

More time talking with James was welcome. I was regurgitating the things Gerhard said to me last night. For some reason talking through it helped, the ideas seemed to form as the words in my sentences did. *But why was I trying so hard to convince myself?*

"James!" Someone yelled, cutting through the silence of the room. A few of my other coworkers looked up with the eruption of noise.

"Hey there," James said after we got a couple of steps closer, "You ready to grab a drink?"

A few people in the group nodded and a woman approached me. We made small talk and danced around different topics, gossiping about all the police around Mendelium and theories about Dave's death. The topic of children came up, and then I noticed a Template device peaking out from beneath her sleeve. Immediately I felt better. Talking with someone distracted me from all the questions bouncing around my head. After brief introductions our group started to leave.

The elevator stopped and the doors opened in front of us.

Anthony stepped off, chin held high, dressed better than anyone else on the floor.

"Charlie," he said. "I was hoping you hadn't left the building yet."

The group of us stopped, everyone looking at me curiously.

"We are on our way out."

"Gerhard needs you in his office," Anthony said, tone demanding. He seemed even less patient than when I'd last spoken to him.

"Why?"

"What do you mean *why*?" he shot back. "His time is more important than yours. He requested you come to his office immediately."

I sighed, "You can let him know I'll be on my way."

"I was asked to bring you myself," Anthony said, continuing with his sour gaze.

"I see," I said, then turned to the group, reaching for my phone, and transferring some money to James. "First round is on me."

He winked back at me. Social interactions weren't my forte, but I knew people liked alcohol and free things. I was a board member now, maybe it was time to learn from James and start investing in relationships.

I got in the elevator next to Anthony. He toyed with his gold cufflinks as the two of us rode up in silence.

Gerhard sat behind his desk across the long, book-clad room. He looked up abruptly, his scowl turned warm as he recognized me.

"Charlie," he said, his toothy smile as white as the clouds floating over the city behind him.

I moved past the sitting area, the fireplace cold and unused today. As much as my eyes had wandered the first time, I'd visited his office I continued to pick out more things scattered across the room. Ornately bound books that looked ancient, and a detailed metal statuette of a man's head exploding into a bouquet of flowers. I resisted the urge to look around further, worried I would stumble into something else in the room. How was he able to navigate this place in his wheelchair?

"Nice to see you again," I said. "What's so urgent?"

"You Charlie," he said nonchalantly, leaning back at his desk. I took a seat at one of the chairs in front of him. I respected the man, but after our walk together I felt a bit less intimidated. He still was *the* Gerhard Geller, CEO of Mendelium. "I've been trying to reach you, I've been in meetings all day, but I wanted to make sure we spoke."

I sat there, not sure what to say, he shared so much last night. Maybe he was hoping to do some damage control or he regretted being so open with me. He would backtrack, I was certain of it. I don't know what game he was playing with me, but it simply didn't make sense that Gerhard would want to do something against the company he founded.

"Thank you again for having Liz and myself over," I said sitting on the edge of my chair.

"It was my pleasure," he said, "but I was hoping we could speak about our after-dinner discussion."

Here it is. *When alcohol brings out a person's true colors why do they so often try to hide from it?*

"I was hoping we could pick up where we'd left off. Have you given my proposition any more thought?"

"I have."

"And?" he sat up straighter in his chair and leaned onto his elbow.

I thought about our conversation last night, remembering the waves lapping up against the shoreline. I imagined myself stepping onto that stage to speak in front of so many people, in each of those moments I felt something inside myself. A focus, like I was doing something that aligned with my being. I felt that again, looking back into the man who held enough power to make the changes I wanted to see in the world. The city moved around behind him, oblivious to how much this conversation could change the trajectory of my life.

"What is it you want from me?" I asked.

"I want you to know I'm serious. It wasn't just words. I am deeply worried what will happen if we continue to let the masses dictate our genetic future. I'm not a fan of talking for the sake of talking, I want to take action. Do you feel the same?"

Well—he certainly didn't call me here to backtrack.

"I do."

"Then we need to decide how to move forward."

"With your position you must be able to sway the public," I said. My apprehension was fading away, the warmth of the drinks I'd felt last night creeping back in. Maybe my defenses were too high. I had no reason to doubt him, but I still couldn't trust the man fully. "I don't think people's minds would change right away, but over time I think we could persuade them."

"Actually Charlie, I was envisioning something more *concrete*," he slid something beneath the palm of his hand on the table. "Are you ready for another promotion?"

He lifted his palm, revealing a security pass with my face on it.

"You and I have very different skill sets Charlie," he began, the lines on his weathered face twisting into a grin. "For this to work we will both need to play a different role. My strengths center around my ability to get a message out to the world, I am capable of changing people's minds." He said it with such confidence. How could someone *know* they could sway the opinions of others?

"What exactly does that leave for me?"

"During your speech you asked for more time. What if there was a way to buy more of it?"

"The Template is slated to begin production in a couple weeks? We're too late."

He gestured for me to grab the security pass. *Charlie Lamarck – Board Seat 17 – Tech Security Specialist.* I rolled it through my fingers, for a brief moment my ego expanded seeing the title printed on the laminated card.

"What if there was a way to revert the Template to the previous version?" he asked. "To put things on pause—just long enough to give us some time."

"Did you have something in mind?" I asked, a growing realization in the pit of my stomach. There was no way this wouldn't come without risk. That was immediately clear upon seeing the security card.

"I had *you* in mind Charlie, I know more about the workings of this company than any other person. But you have a skillset I do not. I understand the people, the genetics, and the production of the Template, but you understand the software. I need you to find a way to sabotage the machine that produces the Template."

Sabotage. That word was terrifying. I thought about Liz, I was no longer making decisions only for myself. I'd allowed emotions to get me into this situation, but this was serious. The stakes were much higher than I'd anticipated. His eyes bore into me from across the desk, there was so much intensity in them, they urged me to agree. *I'd already said yes.* The risks might be insane, but we could change the world, how could I not take it? I could always stop before we did anything illegal.

"If you can find a way to do that, I swear to I will hold up my end of the bargain."

I didn't say anything. I stared at the security card, pretending to be deep in thought. In truth I was trying to breath slowly enough to stop my heart from racing out of my chest.

"With the Template's widespread usage there is constant pressure to ensure the highest level of security around our process. I've appointed you to thoroughly analyze all our security. It will provide the perfect excuse for you to examine all of the inner workings of Mendelium's Template production."

I nodded back at him; the simple action felt consequential. There was a seriousness about Gerhard, he looked at me like I *was* capable of changing the world. "I'll do it."

"It may seem like an insurmountable task, but you have access to every resource I can give you."

I smiled, hoping he wouldn't see the fear in my eyes.

CHAPTER 11

———

"That was divine," Liz said while opening our closet door and taking off her coat. "We don't do dinner as much as we should, just the two of us."

"It's been a month worthy of celebration," I said, walking through our kitchen and following Liz into the living room. The space still seemed too big for us. We wanted enough room for us to grow as a family, but with just Liz and myself the sprawling living room felt indulgent.

"We've been so busy, a successful October deserved a little celebration." After my promotion to the board, I looked like the high achiever of our relationship. This wasn't the case. Elizabeth was the backbone of my own success; she enriched and picked up everyone around her. She'd come so far since the coffee shop, it felt like we'd become different people in these last few years.

She did an animated spin as we walked through the living room, "I can celebrate with the best of them."

I could sense relaxation in the way she moved. With all the stress in my own life it was easy to forget about how much she had in hers. She didn't talk about how much work affected her but managing so many different people and events in tandem was a challenge I could never endure. It was only in moments like this, when she truly seemed carefree, I was able to see how much she normally carried.

"I know you can, I've heard the Elizabeth of old was something to be marveled on the dance floor," I said looking at her with soft eyes.

"Are you calling me old?" she asked playfully.

"I wouldn't dare say something like that," I said as I grabbed her around the waist and kissed her lips, still cool from the crisp fall air.

An intimate dinner and a few drinks made her feel light in my arms. I felt a pang of guilt, I still hadn't told her of my last meeting with Gerhard. In telling her about our stroll along his lake I left out enough details to keep her from knowing how concrete the ideas we discussed were. She looked so carefree, *who was I to take that feeling away from her?* There was no way to speak about my intentions without destroying the entire mood of the evening. We fell on the couch. She came into my arms, the smell of her floral perfume surrounding me. We both looked out towards our backyard, it was dark but lights in the yard illuminated the stone path and plants.

"Life is good right now," she said, I could feel her slowly breathing against me.

"It is."

"Any chance we would have dinner with Gerhard again soon?" She asked, breaking a short silence.

"I don't think so," I said, adjusting and moving around in my seat, "why do you ask?"

"It was refreshing, you know?"

"I enjoyed it too, Gerhard and I had an interesting conversation while I was there, it was not what I was expecting going in but he—"

"No," she interjected, "I mean spending time with Grace."

"What do you mean?"

"Something feels right about it, Charlie... I don't know exactly what it is. Seeing the world through her eyes made me feel something I haven't before. My own life has been so stressful lately, you know how I get, always thinking about the future."

"But you said at dinner that you've been doing so well." *How could I broach this topic while I was considering risking my life?*

"I know what I said," she continued, folding her legs underneath herself and looking at me with wide eyes in the dim light of the room. "It's partly true, things are going well. You are always so happy to be working, you thrive if you have a problem to solve. I worry that you'll keep getting caught up in the next thing and never be ready to settle down and have a family. Dinner with Grace and Gerhard felt like a reset. A reminder. I love children Charlie; I've fought down pressuring you into it for years. I think I'm seeing the missing piece in our lives. I want kids, we've waited so long now, and I don't know if I'm ready to wait much longer."

The dots connected for me, her giddiness on the ride home from the lake, how much she had been asking me about Grace. This conversation came up frequently between us, but much like Gerhard and I's discussion, it no longer felt hypothetical. She looked at me, completely exposed, putting faith in me not to reject her in this moment of vulnerability.

I knew I couldn't think about this right now. Ever since getting my security pass from Gerhard my mind had been swimming with new problems to solve. Learning every detail of production consumed my life, from the vials of nutrient fluid to the servers powering each Template device, I needed to understand every part of this system. The learning and problem solving pushed thoughts of the risks from my mind, but they lurked in the shadows. I could never make a commitment to her while my entire life hung in a balance.

"I'm not ready yet Liz."

Her shoulders fell, she wilted in front of me. "When *will* you be ready?" She asked looking down and away from me, "We keep waiting for the right time, but will things ever be perfect enough for you?"

"I don't know. Right when everything in our lives has changed, my stress has never been higher, it doesn't make logical sense for us to—"

"This doesn't have to be a logical decision Charlie," she said, her posture rigid. "Not everything in life is a problem to solve. This is about you and me. About us. When you are envisioning the future of our relationship what do you see?"

I knew what she wanted me to say, a part of me had always dreamed of having a family of my own. But those weren't the thoughts that crept into my mind in this moment. I imagined our plan with the Template going poorly. I imagined being arrested, going to trial, and spending time in prison away from my new family. I imagined Liz at home with a newborn child, missing the first years of their life because of a decision I hadn't even involved her in.

"I don't know."

"How can you not know that, Charlie?" she shot back. "You *specialize* in thinking about the future. I've seen how much effort you put into the systems you build at work, meticulously planning for each outcome, writing code that takes into account every possible scenario. Can you not do that with *us*? Is a family that far from your mind that you can't even think about it?"

I could see her growing more frustrated as the conversation veered out of control. If I had been honest with her earlier this might not have happened. I just wanted this conversation to be over, I needed some time to finish our plan so I could think straight.

"I just don't think it makes logical sense right this moment. If we can talk about it again in—"

"It's about you, it's about your heart" she said jabbing her finger into my chest. "What do you feel?"

Guilty. Ashamed. I've been dishonest with you and worried that might be causing the rift between us. "I'm not ready yet," I said.

I was so grateful to find a fight that mattered to me. But it wouldn't be fair to bring a child into this world without a father. Moreover, it wouldn't be fair to Liz. I needed more time.

"Let's let things settle down a little bit." I grabbed at her hands, but she pulled them back from me, tears now streaming down her face.

"What do you feel though Charlie? What is your heart telling you?"

I reached my fingers to my neck and felt the pulse of my carotid artery, "Well, it's beating pretty fast, so I think it's telling me I need to relax," I said sarcastically.

Immediately I wished I'd said something else. Her face turned stoic. She dried her tears and stood up with a slow intention, looking down at me. It was a foreign look coming from her. Like the way a mother looks down on a misbehaving child who is oblivious to its own mistakes. She spun around, back to the kitchen, opening the coat closet.

I sat there for a moment, dumbfounded, before leaping off the coach after her. She slammed the door to the garage and the car engine roared to life. I ran out the front door, then barefoot over the cool grass. The taillights trailed off in front of me and I had a realization I was, in fact, feeling something. It felt cold, and it felt like it was all my own damn fault.

CHAPTER 12

EIGHTEEN YEARS EARLIER

The house was silent, and I couldn't have been happier. These couple hours right after school were my favorite. Mom still at work and Dad would be at another doctor's appointment for most of the afternoon. The only sounds were the clicks of my keyboard.

A normal sixteen-year-old might have invited a friend over or done some after school activities. Other parents might worry about leaving their teenage son completely alone at home for a couple hours—but mine knew exactly what I would be up to. My fingers flew across the keyboard, I sipped on an energy drink at the side of my screen, my eyes darting between the blocks of code that poured out of my mind into the editing software.

I'd finished all my coursework weeks ago, but Mr. Kaspowski let me work ahead of the rest of the class, I'd finished up our final project easily, but each day he found more for me to do. At first, I started with simple programs to display messages on the screen, but lately he'd increased the difficulty. I was currently working on an algorithm to find the shortest path between fifty different cities. My fingers danced over the keys, their ridges smooth from my constant use. I looked at all the names of the towns on the list, I wasn't yet sure how to find the optimal route for a car to travel between them. But I knew if I kept trying, I would find the answer. I always did.

I tapped my foot on the ground as I let the code bleed out of me. The shadows of my room grew longer as I intermittently took more sips of my drink. My stomach grumbled. Dad should have been home by now. His treatment appointments usually ended before dinner, I hoped he would grab some takeout on his way home. I enjoyed when he made dinner, but watching him attempt to eat Chinese food with chopsticks was usually more entertaining. He would always get bits of noodles stuck in his mustache. My favorite tradition was opening fortune cookies together and reading each other's cheesy life prediction. I continued on, I'd made so much progress, completely losing track of time. The afternoon faded into the evening. My concept of time pushed away by the challenges of optimizing an algorithm. Sometimes it felt like I teleported into the future, but that's how programming always was for me. My ability to recognize the world around me diminished, I was completely engrossed by the screen in front of me. Out of the window I saw Mom's car pull into the driveway.

I leaned back in my chair, admiring the handiwork. It was remarkable how the problem came together. I'd started with no idea how to solve the problem, and slowly I pieced together smaller parts of the solution. Moments like this felt like magic, maybe anything in life was possible if you could split the problem into small enough chunks? I saved my progress, swiveling around in my chair, then heard the door close downstairs.

"Hey Mom," I shouted as I came down the stairs. "What are we doing for dinner tonight?"

There was no reply. The silence was broken by some rustling downstairs. Movement, but something sounded different about it. I crept down the steps, my mind still ruminating on the code I'd just written. I came to the front door; someone was standing there. My Aunt Linda. Tears streamed down her face.

"Your father," she said, clasping her purse in front of her, breathing heavily. "Something's happened. Your mother asked me to pick you up and bring you to the hospital as quickly as possible."

I didn't know how to respond; I placed my hand on the wall as I felt the world shifting beneath my feet. I stared back at her, not knowing what to say. I steadied myself and walked out the door. I left everything else behind me, my computer spinning away on a problem upstairs. My mind was blank again. I ticced, furrowing my brow, and slamming my eyes shut. I sat in the car seat next to her, as it slowly pulled me toward the hospital. The tics came stronger the closer we got, my entire face shriveling up, I could fight it at first, but I knew it was futile.

I felt in a daze as Aunt Linda guided me through the hospital, being led through sterile hallways, past people in masks, rooms with beeping and other noise to the room that said *Calvin Lamarck*. Then I heard sobbing. My mother hunched over a hospital bed, the face I'd looked up to, the one that always seemed so strong completely broken in front of me.

"Oh Charlie," she said, running across the room and embracing me. Her tears ran across the side of my face, warm down the back of my neck. So far, I'd been able to hold myself together, holding onto hope that Linda had been overreacting to the situation. Seeing Mom weeping broke me. In between the blinking convulsions tears streamed out of my eyes. "What happened?" I asked her, "I thought his treatments had been going so well."

"The doctors still aren't sure," she said, her voice hoarse. "But he's declining quickly."

My father lay there on the bed, his skin pale, like all warmth left him. Mom pushed me towards him. I sensed his exhaustion, he fought to keep his eyes open. He smiled when he saw me, but there was a delay, like he was seeing life just a couple seconds after it happened, "Charles," he said, reaching out a shaking hand. I grabbed onto it, the warmth I wanted to find from it absent. It was as cold as the hospital room. He stared up at me, his deep brown eyes looking into mine, but they were missing something.

"Dad," I said. It was the only word that would come out. I froze, what do you say in this situation, how could I even use words to convey what I was feeling?

"Hey," he said, stroking his hand on my arm, he tried to smile at me, but the pain blunted it.

"I…. I love you so much. You're going to be alright, aren't you?"

"No," he said, tears welling up in his eyes.

I broke down. Watching him wither in front of me, his smile shaking, there was fear in his eyes. I ticced again, so violently tears splashed against his arm. His face hardened, his eyes focusing on me.

"This isn't fair," I said through the tears. "I thought we had more time."

"Listen," he said, "I want you to promise me something. Can you do that?"

I nodded my head. Again, my face convulsing, eyebrows furrowing, eyelids clamping shut. I just wanted them to stop for a moment, to be fully present with my dad.

"Good," he smiled, but it seemed so fragile. He looked at me, speaking with as much strength as he could muster. "I want you to promise me that you'll trust in yourself. No matter what, promise me that you won't listen to them. People will tell you you're different. They will say you have a disability, but they're wrong. Do you understand me? You must learn to love the tics Charlie; they are part of who you are."

I nodded profusely, choking on my words, "I promise, Dad."

The tears still streamed down my face, I clasped both of my hands around his. They were so cold. I just wanted to feel the warmth of his touch again, I wanted to hear his laughter, I wanted to be on the couch next to him at home watching a movie together.

I kept holding on, even after the smile left his face. I kept holding on, even after his gaze drifted away from me. I kept holding on, until the nurses came in and pulled me away from him.

CHAPTER 13

─────

The elevator sunk down beneath Mendelium Tower. The ride was slow, nothing like the massive glass elevators in the main floor. A claustrophobic metal cage. I ticced as I rode down by myself, shrugging my neck and shoulders.

My nerves began to ramp up, I toyed with the security card Gerhard made for me. Thumbing at the title again. *You aren't doing anything wrong.* I told myself, this is *technically* part of my job now. The thoughts didn't calm me at all. The elevator doors opened up in front of me, a burst of cool air poured through the doors.

"We have extra coats down here if you'd like?" said a man wearing a security badge and a jacket. He held it out towards me with a steady smile, his cheeks looked red from the cold. He had a wiry mustache, black with speckles of grey creeping in.

I was taken aback. He reminded me so much of my father, or rather, what my father might look like today if he were still around. I ticced, shrugging my shoulder and neck.

"You must be Charlie Lamarck." he said, "I'm Tim, Vice President of Physical Security. Go ahead, take it, people are never expecting it to be this cold."

I grabbed the jacked and slung it across my shoulders, the fit was good enough. Baggy on my frame compared to Tim's pulling snugly across his midsection. Seeing him made me think about my Mom, I wonder if she ever saw traits of my Dad in the strangers she interacted with. So much changed about our relationship after his passing. Would she have moved away if he was still around today?

I put my hands into the pockets of the jacket, looking around the strange room. As out-of-place as Gerhard's office looked, this room seemed to fit right in. If Mendelium Tower were a futuristic spaceship this would be its heart, the cockpit.

"These servers give off a ton of heat," he said without me prompting. "The racks that hold our systems sit around sixty-eight degrees, but they give off so much heat we have to counteract it somehow. The elevator here is right next to our ventilation ducts."

I looked at the giant opening in the wall, feeling the frigid breeze on the back of my neck.

"I figured it would be cold," I said, looking around the room rather than meeting his eyes. "A lot of the code I've written over the years runs on these machines. I'm looking forward to the tour."

A short stairway descended to an inset floor, with rows of servers that looked like the aisles of a library. Tim walked ahead, leading me down the stairway and into the room. Every row had a metal walkway, each of Tim's steps caused a subtle rattle and creak.

The resemblance to my father was startling. Even his mannerisms were similar.

"This is so much larger than I expected," I said. I felt giddy. It reminded me of when I was a kid opening a box with a new computer. So much data and code flowed through this room. Some people traveled to see the wonders of the world, but in my opinion one of the most impressive marvels sat in front of me. Rows of giant machines, calculating and processing the genetic information of millions of people around the world—all in real time.

"Everyone says that," Tim said stroking at his mustache and gazing across the room," Mendelium holds an astronomical amount of data. Every single person wearing the Template has their data stored in front of you. Their most important health markers are read by the Template then synced with these servers right here. And it doesn't stop when the babies are born, we continue to collect data throughout the child's life. It's *critical* for Mendelium to hang onto this information so the artificial intelligence behind the Template can continually improve."

I took note of the servers, each pulsed with a soft blue glow on the sides, a gentle hum filled the room. I tried to imagine the billions of operations that were happening inside the machines each second, the sheer amount of data flowing in and out of these systems was unfathomable. I had never seen them in person. Each and every one housed more data than I'd ever seen in my life and there were hundreds of them, each working together in unison to power the technological side of Mendelium.

My dad was always so supportive of my programming, but he never got to see all the beauty it brought to my life. Walking through this room, the pinnacle of genetic technology, with a man that reminded me so vividly of him was surreal.

"How long have you been working here, Tim?"

"Since the beginning," he said. "I've spent more time around these machines than my wife and kids at this point.

"How many kids do you have?" I asked.

"Three daughters," he responded, his eyes lighting up. "They outnumber me, but I wouldn't have it any other way. How about yourself?"

"I'm married," I said showing the wedding ring on my finger. "But no children yet, but we are, um, *thinking* about trying soon."

"Well Charlie," he said, that twinkle lingering in his dark brown eyes, "I can promise you won't regret it. Those girls bring me joy every single time I see them. They've all got lives of their own now, but they still make time for their father every weekend. I've even got a new grandson on the way."

I ticced, but smiled back at him through the convulsing, attempting to hide my pain. My dad would have made an amazing grandfather. It wasn't just the feeling of loneliness or the missed birthdays, but all the firsts I never got to share with him that constantly broke my heart. That feeling never actually went away, I'd just grown accustomed to it.

"You must know more about Mendelium's security than nearly anyone," I said.

"I wouldn't say that," Tim said crossing his arms. "They pay people far smarter than me to make sure all of our digital assets are protected. But when it comes to physical security, I'm your guy. I even helped design this room when Mendelium Tower began construction."

"This place looks like a fortress," I said noticing the sheets of thick steel lining the entire ceiling and the massive locks on the elevator.

"It needs to be," he said. "We hold some of the world's most sensitive secrets. Things people wouldn't even share with their closest friends. This building cost billions of dollars to build, but it is worthless compared to what's in this room. Mendelium's true asset is data, the detailed genetic information of millions of people. Information about every Template ever produced, and it's all down here beneath the ground, hidden from the world, completely separate from the rest of the building.

"We have our own independent cooling system, using multiple redundant power generators separate from the ones that power the rest of the building. Even the electrical systems are on a different power source."

Tim gestured up at the ceiling. A fan was installed every few feet and around them lights bearing down on each rectangular machine. "Those fan systems help to pump the heat from the servers out of this room. These ducts don't even go into the central heating exchange in the rest of the building. Both this ventilation system and the one pumping in cold air next to the elevator have their own independent system."

I looked up at them blinking, trying to stay as engaged as possible as he explained the details of the room. I was under the guise of evaluating every aspect of the room, but there was only one specific area that held my interest. He carried on, occasionally motioning to some of the security features that lined the room. I'd already examined the floor plans in detail, but I needed to play my part, diligently listening to his explanations. This room was impenetrable, save for a large metal tube in the back corner. We moved towards it, passing by yet another row of hulking servers.

"You know, you look even younger in person," Tim said. "Most board members are in their forties, especially anyone heading the security panel. You don't look much older than my daughters."

"I can assure you; it was mostly luck. I was just in the right place at the right time."

"Oh, I don't believe that," Tim said as he stroked his mustache. "You don't get promoted to the board without there being an exceptionally good reason."

I knew he was trying to pay me a compliment, but my new position truly wasn't deserved. It felt wrong to lie to him, he seemed so kind and welcoming.

"Thank you," I said, a tic reverberated through my neck and shoulders. He just smiled at me right through it. Some people looked away and pretended not to notice, but he looked back at me with an accepting smile. "I was surprised to be promoted myself, my life has felt like a whirlwind this last month."

"I bet it has," he said, continuing to lead me across the server room floor. We approached the metal tube. It spanned up into the ceiling. Sprouting from the bottom of the pole a collection of thick wires came together like the vines at the bottom of an ancient electronic tree.

"I have to confess," he began, placing his hand on the tube. "I wasn't supposed to be the one giving you a tour today. I heard that you were coming and requested I get the opportunity to show you around."

"Why would you do that?" I asked.

"Well, I was impacted by your speech."

"I see," I said, examining his eyes, they looked so much like my father's. Caring and present. "It was not very well received... clearly."

"I made a point to attend actually," he said. "My youngest daughter has Tourette's syndrome."

"What did you think?"

"I... I don't know what to think. I saw the way she was mocked by her classmates in school. It was brutal. She endured so much ridicule and pain that I wished more than anything I could take away from her. It's a special kind of torture to watch your child be socially berated for being different. If she falls off a bike, I can console her. But teenage girls are devious and harsh, and the kind of pain she was subjected to I couldn't do anything about.

"On the other hand, she is an extremely talented musician. Music always helped with her tics. There is no greater joy as a parent than watching her perform. The tics melt and she gets carried away into the music."

"Programming is like that for me," I said, watching his demeanor relax as he spoke about her.

"I suspected," he said. "I looked you up after your speech, it sounds like your condition brought you a great deal of success. But your symptoms aren't so kind to everyone, when she is performing, she is completely free, but her professional life has been filled with challenges. The stress of interviews always triggers her tics and she's been rejected from countless jobs.

"I'm so sorry," I said, recounting the awkward stares and sideways glances I so often faced throughout my life.

"You don't need to be," he smiled, "I appreciated what you did. I can't imagine how challenging it was to stand up there in front of everyone, your condition on full display."

"Thank you, Tim," I said, nearly forgetting about the metal tube and my task at hand.

"We live in a strange world Charlie, Mendelium saves countless lives with the technology in this room, but what is the cost?"

I smiled back at his brown eyes, I wanted nothing more than to tell him my thoughts, I wanted him to know that others felt the same, but now was not the time. His comfortable demeanor led me to open up more than I should have already. He was right, and I could do something about it.

"I'm sorry Charlie," he said, leaning away from the metal tube. "I didn't mean to talk your ear off. This here is the last stop."

I stepped around the large wires across the floor, all of them funneling into the tube.

"This room was built special," he began, "the cooling and electrical systems are completely separate from the entire rest of this building, with multiple backup generators to ensure redundancy. This tube is the only thing connected to the rest of the building."

I placed my hand against the cool metal. The tube started at the ground and rose all the way up into the ceiling.

He drummed his knuckles against the thick metal, "This thing runs through the entirety of Mendelium Tower. Every floor has connections to it, so programmers like yourself can access our systems when needed. It goes all the way up to the cell tower at this buildings peak, culminating in our own state-of-the-art system to ensure that every mother using the Template has real time communication with these servers."

The system was astounding. As I looked across the sprawling server room, I imagined all of the families who depended on it. Each of the mothers going about their daily activities, the Template working with them to ensure the children in their wombs were developing optimally.

"What happens if it gets disconnected?" I asked, ticcing again through my neck and shoulders.

"Good question," Tim replied, looking past my tics, and connecting with my eyes. "We have multiple levels of redundancy. Every few feet in the tube we have sensors that measure moisture and oxygen levels. If anything suspicious happens, we have backup servers near the cell tower that will fill in temporarily when this system disconnects. The sections of the tube will close, disconnecting it from the rest of the building until we ensure everything is safe."

"And you said *everything* is connected to this?"

"Everything," he said, "from the computers on each floor, the network tower at the top of the building, even the Template production machine itself connects to this system."

Interesting. I began to formulate ideas in my mind. I loved this part, even with just a shred of information a picture started to shape in front of me. Every problem in the world could be solved if you broke it down small enough. I had faith that even a complex riddle like this one could be deciphered. Right now, I just needed more information.

"Are there concerns about being disconnected from the Template production machine? What if that happens during a printing?"

"Another good question," he said, "I'm glad that somebody is taking a more serious look at our security. I think you'll be impressed to know that too would go to our backup systems."

"And those backups... they are always kept up to date with this one?"

"They are often kept on a slightly older version of the system. In case there are any bugs we can easily revert to the last stable version while we make the switch back. On top of that there is so much testing that takes place with the Template, that we've never had a faulty production."

Not yet. "Hopefully that continues," I said with a smile. "I think that's everything Tim. I appreciate you taking the time to show me around."

"I assure you; the pleasure is mine Charlie. I'll have to let my daughter know that I met you, it'll do her some good to see someone flourishing despite their condition."

"I'm still struggling every day," I said, but I could feel my Tourettic brain at work. Any tics were falling away, I had a puzzle to solve, and I had the start of an idea.

CHAPTER 14

———

"I still don't understand this trial run business," Cody said as we paced down the production room floor. He was short and bald, with posture that looked like he lived hunched over the tables in front of us. The room resembled some combination of a laboratory and a manufacturing plant.

"It's not my decision," I said, shaking my head. "Precautions are increasing, it's my job to ensure our security is functioning perfectly. It's set to be the biggest year we've had yet."

Cody gave an animated sigh as he continued to give me a tour of the production floor. The room was hundreds of feet long, with polished concrete floors and fluorescent lights that were beginning to give me a headache.

The room was split in two. The far side was the manufacturing area for the Template device. A wearable electronic patch that constantly communicated with Mendelium's servers. It monitored the nutrient levels in the mother's bloodstream and optimized them in accordance with the server room below.

The other half, the tables in front of Cody and I, were liquid-filled cylindrical glass vials, suspended in each were hundreds of different nutrients, minerals, and drugs designed to be administered during critical points of their pregnancy. Looking around I marveled at the level of technological synchronicity required to get this to work. So many systems, medical and technological, stacked on top of each other.

He gestured to the machine in front of us, "One of you big wigs upstairs makes a call and now I have to tell all my guys they are required to work overtime. I struggle enough to find good help, I had one of my best workers quit this week because of it."

The fault was my own. This entire trial run was deemed necessary to reevaluate the security of the Template, but only Gerhard and myself knew the actual reason. I needed to get eyes on our testing process. My mind was alive with ideas for how to revert the Template, but I was missing something, I hoped to find it here.

We walked past the rows of tables lined with the Template vials, I picked one up and examined it more closely. Inside of each where hundreds of smaller tubes, each with different color liquids. Different substances that would be necessary during each stage of the pregnancy.

"The board can send you down to watch, bark orders, or whatever it is you intend on doing. But it's not going to make any difference," Cody grumbled. "My men refuse to put in any more overtime."

I continued to play with the vial in my palm, "That's actually the opposite of why I'm down here Cody. I just cleared it with Gerhard, your entire team can go home early today and have the rest of the week off. You've went above and beyond, and the entire board is grateful for your sacrifice."

"Oh," he said, turning to me, his hunched posture straightening. "I'll look forward to letting my team know."

I smiled as he turned away from me, continuing the tour, with a little more lightness in his step. Getting them some time off was the least I could do considering I'd subjected them to more work. They were just pawns in a larger plan, but I couldn't let myself think of them that way. All these workers around me had their own families and lives they were excited to get home to. No matter how much Gerhard and I's plan would benefit the world, I mustn't lose sight of the helping the people around me right here and now.

"How do you test these?" I asked, still toying with the glass Template vial in my hand.

"We use a scanner," he said. "I can show you if you like?"

"Please."

We approached a metal door near the middle of the giant production room, Cody pulled out a keycard and placed it beneath the scanner. A green light flickered, and he pulled the handle.

"I still don't see why any of this is necessary," Cody said as he led me across the storage room and toward a cabinet on the other end. "We've never had a defect released to the public; our system has worked without fail for years."

Well, you've never been tested, I thought as Cody opened the large cabinet, using his keycard again. The entire height of the cabinet was lined with small black devices, each with a connector port and a screen.

"That's all of them?" I asked, "I thought there would be hundreds with how many Template vials are produced in the facility."

"This is plenty," Cody said flatly, "We don't even end up using all of them, reasonable levels of accuracy and all that."

"How many people does it take to scan them?"

"Oh it's a few of us, and we only manually test around one percent of the product, barring there aren't many hiccups."

"Are those... hiccups, usual?" turning over and examining the scanner in my hands.

"We've had a faulty batch or two each year, but we've always caught em," Cody said proudly. "They say our standard of excellence is one of the reasons Mendelium has been so successful. If that's true you'd think they'd pay us more."

I smiled, but didn't take my eyes off of the device, its screen lit up in front of me with a prompt to attach a vial.

"How do they work?" I asked.

"Nothing much to it. Just attach a vial to the port and it'll scan the liquid. It'll test all of the various compounds, if something is off it flashes a big red X and we know to examine things more closely."

I continued nodding along with him, "I need to take this one, the board wants me to examine every part of our quality assurance process closely, even down to the scanners. What about security for this area?"

"We have extensive camera systems across all of the entrances and full-time guards on staff during production."

That wasn't a problem for right now. I pushed that portion of the plan into another part of my mind. Life is kind of like code, just solve one problem first, then the next. I had done what I said I would, that was all for today.

I'd investigated things, even got my hands on a scanner—but seeing the cameras made it feel real. A single piece of evidence could bring my life toppling down. *For what?* People still lined up to purchase the Template at record rates. I thought speaking of my beliefs in front of a crowd might help me to find closure, but it did the opposite. It reminded me how much I cared, it reminded me how confident I was in my beliefs.

When I spoke with Gerhard, I felt immune to any repercussions, hopefully seeing him would inspire more confidence than I felt down on the production floor. I took the scanner, traversing the towering building up to the 100th floor.

Things were beginning to feel so *real*. Liz still didn't know, and I was too far to turn back now. I still felt a void in our relationship, but there was only so many areas I could focus.

His office had grown on me, something about the long room with beautiful wooden bookcases felt like home. It seemed lived in. The room had the comfortable feel of a small den with a warm fireplace. Golden light illuminated the back half of the room where we were sat.

"Take a look at this," I said, passing the black scanner across the table.

He rolled it over in his good hand, "What is it?"

"One of the scanners they use for testing the Template."

He turned it on, the white light illuminating the weathered lines of his face. He looked older today. Exhausted. I wonder if the anxiety that was eating away at me was beginning to phase him.

"And you think you'll be able to edit the code?"

"Possibly."

He looked up at me from the scanner, his green eyes cold and calculating.

"I have an idea," I continued. "Hold down the power button and the scanner trigger at the same time."

He obliged, still looking confused. "What is this?" He asked after the white light illuminating his face shifted to a blue.

"That's my way in."

CHAPTER 15

————

EIGHTEEN YEARS EARLIER

I sat in the back of the classroom, behind my class-mates' judgmental eyes. It had been two weeks since the hospital. The pain was as fresh today as every day before. The only respite was the first minutes after waking up, a few seconds of time before realizing my life would never be the same, no matter what I did I could no longer get back to the life we'd had. He used to wake me up, tell me to get ready for school, we'd talk about the day over our morning pancakes. I hadn't eaten breakfast in days. The old routine reminded me too much of him. Better to avoid it.

Today started the same, lying in bed dreading the day ahead of me, dragging myself to school. I ticced. The same eyebrow furrowing contraction, the one that came about on that terrible day still stuck with me. The tics always frustrated me, but this one served as a reminder. Each time my face spasmed I saw the way my dad looked at me, his eyes slipping farther and farther away.

The teacher did attendance, the noises of the class seemed distant. I'd been so disconnected from school, attendance was the only thing I could do right these days.

"Charlie," the teacher said from behind her desk.

"Here," I said, head propped up on my arm, leaning heavy on the desk. There were some snickers around the classroom, and a couple of the kids looked back at me.

"I see that," she said. "We are starting off reports with you today, you can go as soon as you're ready."

Shit. I'd completely forgotten the report due today. I'd been forgetting a lot of things lately. It didn't matter, there was no use putting this off, she'd already given me two extensions. I'd been dragging myself through every other element of my life lately, there was no reason I couldn't drag myself through this speech. Most of the teachers had been giving me space since Dad died, but my free pass had ended.

I pulled myself up out of my chair, dragging my feet through the aisles of desks. The teacher pulled up the slides I'd prepared on the screen. I barely remembered putting it together, but there it was. Each member of the class had to give a report on how World War II affected European countries. My first slide showed the flag of Poland and a picture of the Auschwitz-Birkenau concentration camp.

I readied myself, breathing in and out slowly, trying to pace myself. I'd done this before; I could do it again. My face convulsed. I had to start; I couldn't let the tics slow me down.

"On September 1st, 1939, Nazi Germany invaded Poland, triggering the start of World War II. By the end of the first month, after heavy shelling and bombing, Warsaw surrendered to the Germans. At the same—"

I ticced aggressively. Losing my train of thought, my whole head jolting forwards against my own will. Smiles spread across the class.

Just ignore them.

"At the same time the Soviet Union invaded eastern Poland. The last resistance ended on October 6th. Poland would remain under German occupation until January 1945. For the remainder—"

I ticced again. They came faster now; I'd never felt them so strong. My head snapping forward at the same time my eyes and face twisted.

"For the remainder of the war—"

Again. Worse than before. The smiles turned into laugher, my momentum gone, I looked back at my slide trying to remember what came next. I clicked the button to go to the next slide. Nothing happened. The teacher shot a glare at the students who were barely holding it together. I tried it again, still nothing happening on the screen.

"For the remainder of the war—"

Again, I spasmed. This time some of the boys in the class began to mock me, snapping their heads forward, contorting their eyes and faces, every couple seconds. *Was that really what I looked like?* I ticced again, still as bad as ever. Never had they been this out of control, faster and more disruptive.

"The Nazi party—"

I snapped again, launching me back into the hospital. Feeling them just as I had on that day. The other boys and the class continued copying me, snapping their heads forward, even some of the girls were laughing now. I imagined my father looking at me, was this how I looked to him as he lay there dying? I was his broken son. Was it pity I saw in his eyes in those final moments? His last words weren't even I love you. He saw right then what I was, even my own father couldn't look past my syndrome. I ticced again, this time tears coming with them.

The laughter echoed through the classroom. The boys all slamming down their eyes, copying me. I turned around. I couldn't look at them anymore, I didn't want them to see the tears streaming down my face, it was too late.

"Stop it, all of you!" The teacher yelled, but it hardly mattered. I ticced again; it wasn't just the spasm anymore. Each tic brought me back beside the hospital bed. Back to the father I no longer had.

I rushed out the door, face buried in my hands. I ran. Speeding through the hallways, wiping off my face on the way. Passing a teacher who asked where I was going, but I just ignored them. I turned a corner, down through the stairwell, weaving my way through the entire school. The empty halls reminded me of the hallways of the hospital with their fluorescent lights beating down overhead. I reached Mr. Kaspowski's room and pulled open the door. The whole class looked up at me from their computers, and Mr. K spoke from the front of the class.

".... keep working on the problems for now. I'll stop by and check on you shortly."

He walked over to me, guiding me into a seat away from the peering eyes of the class.

"What's wrong Charlie?" He asked. He knelt and placed his hand on my shoulder, his grey eyes examining me through wire rimmed glasses.

I ticced again. I'd hoped they would fade into the background when I wasn't in front of the class, but they were just as out of control now.

"I just needed to get away," I said between convulsions. My face was beginning to grow tired, my muscles exhausted, but there was no end in sight. "I wanted something to distract me. Can I use one of your computers?"

He placed his hand into the pocket of his khaki pants "This is the key to my office. I want you to take it and use my personal computer. You can stay in there as long as you'd like."

I grabbed it from him and bolted into the office, closing the door and powering on the machine. I broke down, crying in the room filled with scattered books and paper. The computer powered on. I opened a textbook to the homework assignments in the back. One in particular looked appealing, designing an algorithm to solve the Rubik's cube. It didn't matter what it was, I just needed something to distract me, a single thing in my life I could actually control.

I opened the editor and began. Allowing my mind to descend into the code. I broke the problem into chunks, solving for smaller parts of the whole. First creating a sequence of moves to reorient corner pieces, then one to swap the location of two different colored edge squares. I stepped through from one to the next, continuing to move forward, not letting my mind go to anything else. I got it working, but my work still wasn't finished. I cleaned it up, refactoring the code, reorganizing my ideas. My fingers glided across the keyboard, the sounds of the classroom nonexistent.

There was a gentle knock on the door, I pulled my consciousness away from the problem at hand. Back into the real world.

"Hey honey," my mom said. Mr. Kaspowski looked over her shoulder, the room was completely empty now. I looked over at the clock—school had been out for three hours. I didn't have any words, I'd escaped temporarily, but the emotions were back. I wrapped my arms around her, and the tears came back again.

CHAPTER 16

———

The hairs stood up on the back of my neck, as the officers looked in my direction. I hoped their eyes wouldn't linger. They didn't, they were as oblivious to me as I was of their investigation.

Police were common at Mendelium Tower these days. There was no new information about Dave's death, but security increased dramatically. The checkpoints always had extra staff and officers were constantly hanging around the main entryway. They must be here for a reason. *Perhaps his death wasn't as straight forward as it first seemed?* I'd been cautiously waiting for them to approach me, I looked forward to it, I wanted to get more information about the investigation.

As long as it wasn't today. Most of my coworkers had already been interviewed about their relationship to Dave. Liz didn't learn much when she was questioned, her entire staff had to go into the station and give statements about what they saw on the night of the party.

It hurt a little thinking about her, that area of my life felt slightly off kilter. I'd apologized. We made up. But underneath each of our small interactions lay tension. An unspoken void hung between the two of us. I needed to find some way to right the situation, some time had helped, but she deserved better than me waiting for the problem to fade away.

I quieted my mind, right now there was a problem to solve.

I moved through the crowds on the first floor, past the elevator and around towards one of the entrances for maintenance staff. I looked back one more time at the officers, checking again for any eyes in my direction. None. I stepped through the door, the echoing murmurs of the crowd and sunlight of the sprawling entry way closed with the door behind me. The polished granite floors and ivory walls turned to grimy tile, the smells of bleach emanating through the hallway. I crossed paths with someone who worked in the kitchen, nodding as we walked off in different directions.

Gerhard's idea to have me focus on security was brilliant. No one batted an eye as I moved through the storage areas and back rooms, I was able to go anywhere in the building, to ask any questions without worry of being conspicuous. It's incredible how many places you can get into with a confident stride and a professional looking badge.

In the movies a hacker sits in their white van. Dramatic music revs up the tension and the audience gasps as they cut off the camera system just in time to prevent them from being revealed. The reality couldn't have been more different. I weaved through

Mendelium Tower's back hallways like a computer virus parsing through a hard drive, but I wrote all the code last night, in my comfortable pajamas with a warm cup of tea. No black hoodie. No bypassing of alarm systems.

I looked around the kitchen, trying not to linger in any one place for long. The greasy smells of the food followed me all the way down the hallway, I turned into a bathroom before I crossed paths with a group of people. I stood there near the door, waiting for the sound of them passing by. Holding my bag close, still not accustomed to the heavy weight inside. I pulled out my phone, referencing again the map of the first floor. I seemed so far from the production room in these back hallways, but it was only fifty or so feet ahead of me. There should be some kind of storage closet up ahead.

I left the bathroom and walked on, rounding a corner, and entering the door before I crossed paths with anyone else wandering these hallways. The room was dark and didn't have the stale smell of the small storage closet I was expecting. I fumbled around, pawing at the wall until my finger connected with a light switch. *It's so clean.* I was hoping for more dust, a well-kept room would mean it was used more often. The last thing I wanted was for someone to come in here and find me.

There were two doors against the far wall. Between them a collection of bins, with some sort of labeling on them. I walked past some chairs, examining the label on the first. *Alonso, Samuel.* I looked to the other bins; each with a name printed on it. I opened the first, inside was some candy, medication bottles, and a lunch box. I noticed the television screen mounted to the wall and the chairs I'd walked past facing it. *Shit. It's a break room.*

I pulled out my phone again, first checking the time. *11:29.* Most workers in the building started their lunch at noon, hopefully that would leave enough time.

I pulled up the map. I ticced, my eyes snapping shut and face twisting. I opened the left door, stepping through into a closet. *It should be just past here.* I looked around all the walls, moving aside the coats and clothing hanging up until I found it. A small metal panel hidden tucked inconspicuously in the corner. Locked. Accessible only to those with the proper clearance card. My new ID badge would unlock it, but I couldn't risk that. Every time employees used the badge to open something it was recorded, stored down in a database on one of the massive servers in the basement. Sneaking through back hallways was a new experience for me, but I understood the power of data. A single database record saying I was here could bring my entire life toppling down. I'd successfully evaded the eyes of my coworkers, I would have to hide from the computer systems as well.

In computer programming, there is something called a brute-force algorithm, where the programmer relies on the computers processing power rather than their own intelligence to solve a problem. Rather than getting fancy and optimizing the code, you let the computer do the heavy lifting. Computer processes work so fast that, even though it's not optimal, it doesn't matter. Sometimes, rather than a brilliant solution, it was better to rely on the machine. That's exactly how I felt now as I pulled the drill from my bag. I got here, now wasn't the time for more lies or thinking, it was time to let the machine work.

I attached the hole saw bit to the drill and turned it on. I winced at the seemingly thunderous sound as the bit slowly cut through the wall. Then I set the circular piece of drywall to the side, then attached the long metal bit onto the drill. I peered into the hole and saw what I was looking for, the same as the large metallic tube I saw downstairs. Less than forty feet from where I'd examined it with Tim days prior. Even closer to the Template production machine, connected to the other side of this wall.

This next moment worried me. It was secluded, but the noise of a drill could attract attention. I ticced again, convulsing, then pushing my glasses back up to their place. I breathed out and pulled the trigger. At first, I didn't think it was working, it screeched as it spun on the metal, but within a second it caught. Slowly I depressed the trigger, pushing harder against the metal. My heart pounded in my chest, had I measured properly? I knew the dimensions, but if any variable was incorrect, I would fail. Even touching one of the pressure pads would trigger an alarm in the server room. Push too hard and the drill might damage one of the wires housed within, triggering an alarm and bring the plan slamming down to a halt. Slowly I pushed, sweat now forming at my brow, my arm grew tired from holding the drill at an awkward angle.

I broke through. Letting off at just the right time, I relaxed my hand and waited. No noises. No talking.

No alarms. Relieved, I rested my head against the wall for a moment, still fearful of someone finding me. I needed to work fast. From my bag I grabbed the small plastic tubing, I placed it into the hole formed by the drill. I taped a seal around it, then grabbed the container of water from my bag, inserting it through the hole and attaching it to the tube. I held the bag's release clamp with my fingers while I grabbed the last item from my bag—a small device I'd programmed the night before.

It was magnetic and attached inside the tube. Simple, but effective. It was only compromised of a few parts; a magnet, a clamp, and a minicomputer chip I'd programmed myself. The program was easy enough for me to design, all it would do is connect to the Mendelium network and wait. I manually clamped the device shut around the water bag, carefully removing my fingers ensuring that it took. As long as my phone was attached to the network I could access the device. A push of my finger and my phone would notify the device to open, releasing the water down into the metal tube. An alarm would trip when it recognized an unexpected substance, protecting the server room, and causing the servers to revert to the backup system.

I smiled. This was the moment I loved so much about what I did. The countless keystrokes and mental fatigue were always worth it at the end. I'd built something, an idea that formed in my mind now existed in the real world. My brain, no matter how much it made me look like a freak, created something new. If that isn't magic, I don't know what is.

Slowly I placed the circular piece of drywall back into its place. Cautiously applying putty and paint around the cuts to cover my tracks. Finding the paint was almost more challenging than setting up the device. I'd spent evenings combing through Mendelium Tower's construction records to find the exact shade used in this area of the building.

I sat back and examined my handiwork; from a distance you couldn't even tell the wall had been accessed. I wiped down the area, ensuring I left no sign of myself here. I moved the coats back into their respective places, tossing my gloves back into the bag.

Voices in the hallway grew louder. I exited the closet into the break room, hurrying to get to the door. I waited there for a moment, as the people approached. I ticced, the side of my face jerking, quickly formulating an excuse for why I would be here.

But they passed. Again, fortunate to avoid prying eyes. I left the room, each stride down the hallway felt like it carried me twice as far. The more space I placed between the break room and myself the more confident I became, by the time the elevator reached my floor I was euphoric. The receptionist smiled and I tried my hardest to keep my emotions closed off. I walked past the offices of my coworkers, none of them knowing any different.

I approached my own office door and noticed the door ajar.

Every step I took today was meticulous. Every part of the plan thought through and diligent, there is no way I would have forgotten to close it. I stepped inside, someone sat in one of the chairs.

"Hey hun," Liz said. "Where have you been?"

CHAPTER 17

———

"Um," I paused, waiting for the words to come. The lies I'd rehearsed for my coworkers wouldn't work here. I broke the law. Gerhard and I's plan was not an idea any longer, and the woman who deserved to know more than anyone else still didn't. "What are you doing here?"

"You said you wanted to have lunch this week," she said, examining the shocked expression on my face. "Well, here I am."

I smiled back, but it felt strained, there was no use, she could always see through me. "Sorry, I completely forgot, it's been such a busy morning."

"Are you doing alright?" she asked, standing up from the chair and placing both her hands on the sides of my arms, her dark blue blouse highlighting her eyes. She looked up at me, examining. Did she find what she was looking for? Just feeling her touch was comforting, I'd experienced such a wide array of emotions in the last hour I didn't know what to think of her sitting in my office. Carefully I placed my bag down behind my desk, attempting to draw as little attention to it as possible.

"Honestly Liz, I don't know, this morning has already felt like a lifetime."

She bit her bottom lip and reached down to grab her bags, "It's alright Charlie, I understand, I should have called first to make sure you would have—"

"No," I said, cutting her off. I grabbed her wrist and pulled her in close to me, "my brain has been moving a thousand miles an hour, but there is nothing else in the world I'd rather do than get out of here and spend some time with you."

I ran my finger through her hair, pulling her into a kiss. Her lips gently locking with mine, the world moving slowly for a moment. It always did with her. This room could grow cold with all the time I spent working in it, but with Elizabeth it felt comfortable in a way no decor could imitate.

She smiled up at me. "No lunch at your desk today then?"

"Absolutely not. How about the park?"

"I'd love to."

We left Mendelium Tower behind. Away from the double-helix behemoth, and out into the rest of the city. Cars shot past us, and crowds of people pushed through, dressed in whatever corporate costumes they were required to wear. The day was brisk but refreshing. We walked slowly down the sidewalks towards the park, holding hands like we did during our early dates. How was it I always forgot about the simple things? The touch of my wife, the rays of the sun warming my face. Life seemed so hectic an hour ago, but here with the woman I love time moved the way it should, as slow as the fall breeze.

We entered the park, like an oasis from the synthetic desert of the city. The leaves were vibrant, the sounds of the river an escape from the bustling noises of the metropolis . The crisp air expanded deep into my lungs. Liz looked radiant in front of it all.

"It's the perfect time of year," she said, pushing her hair over one shoulder. "When the leaves are just starting to change. Not so late that all the green is gone, but far enough along that each tree has its own unique shade. It's the only time you can truly see the forest's character. The oak trees make—"

"I wasn't working when you came into the office today. Something's happened I haven't been able to bring myself to tell you."

She turned toward me; the look of awe fell from her face.

"Do you remember the walk Gerhard and I took after dinner? He was more receptive to my speech than I anticipated. And…"

She stared back at me, the expression on her face unreadable. Her eyes locked onto mine, urging me to continue.

"…we put a plan into action. Gerhard shared many of the frustrations with the Template as I did. I know it sounds crazy, I put everything we have at risk. If Gerhard can play his role as well as I've played mine perhaps, we can even change a few minds."

"I don't follow," she said, gaze steady.

"We are reverting this year's Template so Tourette's syndrome isn't eliminated."

"That's.... *terrifying*," she said, "Are you aware of how many people's lives you are affecting? Can you just do something like that?"

"We already are. I've been feeling so guilty not telling you, a part of me thought that if I didn't say anything, it would make it less real."

"Not only did you make a decision for millions of people, but you did it behind my back. What do you expect me to say to that?"

"I don't know Elizabeth. I never wanted to put you in this position. If I didn't do something meaningful when I have the chance what does that make me? I love you, Liz. I love our life together. But I don't know how I could live with myself if I didn't do *something*. For years I've hated myself over the decision to sell out to Mendelium. I was in a position to change hundreds of people's lives and I chose wrong. I won't let myself make that mistake again. I must do what I believe in, even if it is the hard choice. I've learned so much about myself since then, I've learned so much from you. I have to have faith in myself to make the decisions I know are right."

She smiled. *Why was she smiling?*

"So, this is why you've been acting strange. These last few weeks you've seemed so... different. I thought your new role at Mendelium was suiting you, this makes more sense. You had a new problem to solve."

"You're not mad?" I asked.

"I'm furious, Charlie. You've been keeping a huge secret from me, and we are nowhere near done talking about it. At this moment however, I'm glad I finally understand what has been happening with you. Not knowing has been driving me crazy."

"I love you," I said, the words felt like they erupted out of me from nowhere. Why did I ever think it would be a good idea to hide something like this from her? She's always been supportive. I embraced her in a hug, her warmth a reprieve from the cool breeze that rustled the leaves of the park.

"I love you too," she said. "You can always be honest with me Charlie. Always."

"I was just on the first floor, setting up a device to undermine the Template production."

I gazed back at her face, looking for anything in her eyes to tell me how she felt. Analyzing every small movement on her face like a computer parsed a file. Everything would hang on this moment. I hated keeping it from her, but I couldn't risk her turning me down. It was too late to disapprove, but if I didn't have Liz on board there was nothing I could do. She looked away from me, out across the stream running through the park.

"I'm not finished yet," I continued. "I swear to you I will be as careful as possible. Gerhard has my back completely; we are working together."

"What if something goes wrong? What would happen to you?"

"I don't think we should think about that."

"How can you ignore it?" she shot back, "It's not just about *you*, Charlie. How can we start a family if you are in prison?"

"Liz," I said, placing my hand on her shoulder. "I've been self-centered, I should have talked to you first. All you have to do is say the word and I will stop. If it is what you want, I'll tell Gerhard I'm done."

"No," she said. "What kind of wife would I be if I forced you to stop doing something you believed in?"

"A perfectly justified one. This is insane, Liz."

"You just have to be careful. Can you promise that? Can you make sure that Gerhard does everything in his power to keep you safe?"

The park behind her now seemed even more vibrant, the blue sky above more saturated with color. A weight lifted from my chest, the tension in my jaw loosened. She approved. I didn't have to continue living a lie.

"You can tell him yourself if you like," I said.

She looked up at me, beautiful and confused, "You want to walk up into his office and tell him to talk to your wife? You really think one of the busiest men in the world has time for that?"

"Well, he has time enough to take his daughter to the park and eat ice cream," I said and nodded towards the park bench behind her.

Grace ran around the bench feeding pigeons, throwing bits of bread while they swarmed and fought over the pieces. Gerhard sat to the side of the bench, his electric wheelchair shining in the sunlight. He wore the same relaxed smile he had back at home. Grace brought out a softer side of him.

"Charlie and Elizabeth Lamarck," he said as we approached. "What brings you to the park today?"

"Liz and I had a lunch date," I said, "it is such a beautiful day we had to come outside and enjoy it together. How about you two?"

"The pigeons of course," Gerhard said, gesturing at Grace. "Birds are her newest obsession. I told her that we have a wide variety of species back at home, but she insists that the pigeons that live in the city are the most interesting."

Grace squatted down with a fist full of bread she'd begun to crumble and toss to the birds, watching each of them move with her head cocked to the side.

"Grace, why don't you come over here and say hello to Charlie and Liz."

She didn't respond, her attention too wrapped up in examining the pigeons, she looked completely overjoyed to be there. She wore purple jeans and a wool coat that hung a just little too far down over her hands. Gerhard sighed looking mildly frustrated, but underneath that I sensed a proudness in him as he watched the birds mingle in front of her. A ringing noise came from Gerhard's pocket, cutting through the natural noises of the park.

"I need to take this," he said, "do you think the two of you could help watch Grace for a couple minutes while I take a call?"

"Of course," Liz said enthusiastically, "we would love too."

Gerhard wheeled over to Grace, causing many of the pigeons to fly away, and whispered to her. She seemed upset for a moment but smiled towards us. Gerhard rolled his chair away from us, and Grace ran over to the bench and sat down.

"Are you a bird lover too?" Liz asked.

Grace's eyes grew wide, "They are so cool, pigeons are much smarter than people give them credit for, did you know they can find their way back home from thousands of miles away?"

"Really?" Liz said. "That's impressive."

"Ya," Grace said, turning and looking back towards the birds. The flock was starting to cautiously come back towards the crumbs of bread laying on the cement. "I don't think my dad likes them very much though. He hangs out with me in the park, but he never wants to feed the birds."

"His loss," I said, and gestured my hand towards the birds. "Do you mind?"

She shook her head and smiled back at me. Taking a piece of bread out of her coat pocket and handing it to me. I crouched down to her level and tossed the crumbs, the birds scrambled onto the new pieces, their heads bobbing back and forth all around us.

"You know Grace," I began, "you should tell your dad that his company wouldn't exist if it weren't for pigeons just like these. Darwin was obsessed with pigeons, breeding a whole flock of them at home, if it wasn't for those pigeons he might never have come up with his theories of evolution. If it wasn't for him, and his friendly birds, companies like Mendelium wouldn't be around today. Pigeons are part of the reason he has a job."

Her face lit up, smiling ear to ear. Her cheeks rosy in the cold air.

"Can I show you some of my drawings of birds sometime? We have hundreds around our house, I even have names for a few."

"I would love that," said Liz as she looked over at me with a heartwarming smile. She really did seem to enjoy spending time with Grace. The high per-forming party-planning Elizabeth was still there, but underneath it another layer I wasn't as accustomed to seeing. I wonder if she saw the same thing in me.

"Where are your kids?" Grace asked Liz, she seemed to be out of bread and was starting to focus her interest more towards the two of us than the birds.

"We don't have any yet," Liz said.

"Not yet? Do you plan to have some soon, then?"

"We do," I said, looking at Liz, lingering on her eyes and for a brief moment.

"Good," Grace said, "you both seem nice, and it's a waste if you don't have any kids to be nice to."

"Well," Gerhard said as he rolled his wheelchair back towards us. "I see you three got along just fine. How about it, Grace? Are you ready to head back and let these two enjoy their lunch?"

"Actually," Liz said. "I was hoping that you and I could have a discussion."

"Ok," Gerhard said with some apprehension. Liz led him away again, leaving Grace and I on the park bench.

"What do you think they're talking about?" Grace asked.

"Me," I said, smiling at her. Grace and I continued to toss pieces of bread to the birds, all the while I stole glances towards the two of them. One of the most powerful men in the world, and Liz still seemed confident and commanding. His face was stern and his eyes wide, a look that seemed out of place on his face. Even from a distance Liz's words looked sharp, she stood, firmly planted to the ground and spoke her mind. It was a side of her I wasn't used to, a brash drive she normally reserved for her work, but she let it loose. I couldn't believe that less than a month ago Gerhard was someone who intimidated me, in reality it was my wife who deserved my regard.

"She looks angry," said Grace, who had now joined me at watching the two of them speak back and forth. I tried as hard as I could to catch some of the conversation, but the constant rustle of wind through fall leaves muffled any snippet I caught. I turned away. What else could I do? I trusted them both, and I needed them both in a different way. Anxiety bubbled inside me, a feeling I'd been growing so accustomed to lately. I looked away pretending to be interested in the birds again.

"They are coming back over," Grace said, smiling at me. "Be cool."

As much as Liz and I spoke of having children, I only ever thought of them being babies. Grace was something I didn't understand, but that was exciting. She had so much personality, so many interests and passions, I could only hope that in the future, Liz and I would be able to enjoy moments in the park like this with children of our own.

"Your wife is particularly persuasive," Gerhard said.

"He knows that better than anyone," Liz said, a knowing smile plastered across her face.

"You are fortunate to have someone in your life that cares for you in the way Liz does."

She looked at me, hands on her hips, looking satisfied.

"What do you say? Do you two want to come with Grace and I to eat some lunch?"

"We'd love that," I said. Grace tossed the last of her bread to the birds, they swarmed again, looking curiously towards the young girl who'd been feeding them so well. She followed along behind him, his wheelchair barreling ahead in front of us. I hung back, hoping to put a little bit of space between Gerhard and us.

"What did you say to him?" I whispered.

"I told him what you said I should."

"And what was that?"

"That if anything at all happened to you, I would do everything in my power to make his life a living hell."

She looked back at me, her eyes as beautiful as ever, something looked different in them. A fiery self-assurance lurked behind their light blue facade.

CHAPTER 18

ONE YEAR EARLIER

A suit and tie and a press conference, was there a worse combination? I pulled at my tie, cranking my head to the side as I did it—a new tic forming in real time. Cameras pointing at me was stressful enough, but this silk noose around my neck was suffocating.

Gerhard spoke to the reporters. We were told to smile in the background as they interviewed him. He spoke eloquently, the most recent release was hugely successful—in large part because of the GeniSense acquisition. Everyone else seemed happy for the recognition, but as I sat in the background, adjusting my tie and cocking my head to the side, I thought about who truly deserved this credit—my old team at GeniSense. They'd all moved on with their lives, but watching Gerhard take credit for something we'd built brought on those feelings again. I let them down.

Their work and recognition went to people at Mendelium who didn't even know their names. I tried my best to smile as the cameras focused on Gerhard's carefully rehearsed words. Out of the stress and frustrations only came more tics.

The day passed by much like any other, but a layer of regret lurked in the background of my mind. I continued to work, plugged into my new role as a cog in the gigantic genetic machine. Just a single block of code in a monolithic server. At least our work meant something, we helped to rid the world of crippling diseases, we made people's lives easier. It changed the world in a positive way—maybe my ego was getting too involved—who cares who took the credit for it, our efforts helped people across the globe.

I walked through the hallways, finishing my early morning session of architecting a new piece of software for the Template's distribution. As always, the time flew by as I let my consciousness wrap around the challenges, finding a way to solve my problems with code. A group of people huddled around the desks in the middle of the floor, a couple of them chuckling. Their laughter felt out of place. Mendelium's tech floor was typically quiet, the engineers were always busy and the higher ups were too swamped with their own work to bother with water cooler conversations. I continued my walk, a little bit of movement helped me think.

I crossed paths with some of the new interns. Each of them looking at me in turn and snickering. I brought my hand up to my face, wiping it clean. I looked down at myself to make sure I hadn't spilled something on my shirt. There was something behind their tight-lipped smiles, a joke that I wasn't in on. James walked across the floor, directly towards me.

He walked up cautiously, inspecting my face. *Somethings happened.* He placed his hand on my shoulder, "Hey C, how are you holding up?"

"Fine," I said.

"Do…do you have a moment to chat?"

"Sure."

"Let's go to your office," he said, looking across the room. As he did a couple sets of eyes darted away from us. I followed him, again checking my appearance. I stood behind my desk, and he closed the door behind him.

"Have you seen it yet?" He asked sternly.

"What?"

"The video."

I just shook my head, "Of what?"

"The press conference."

"It's up already?"

He nodded slowly. Something felt off, his charm and smile replaced with cautious eyes and tight lips. "Look, I don't know how to say this, someone caught a video of you ticcing in the background, people on the internet picked it apart."

"Who?"

"Does it matter? Look Charlie, I'm sorry, is there anything I can do for you? If you want to go out and grab a drink and get away from here, I would totally understand."

"I want you to show me the video."

"I really don't think it's necessary…" he began but trailed off when I glared at him. Begrudgingly he pulled it up. The original shot looked focused on Gerhard, but this one was zoomed in. Focused squarely on me. I saw myself, grabbing onto the tie and yanking my head to the side. It set in slowly, the terrible realization that the tic was stronger than I even recognized. I grew so accustomed to them that I forgot just how abrupt and unusual they would look to another person. I ticced again now, reaching to the side of my collar, feeling just how much my neck pulsed.

Beneath the video, my eyes darted down into the comments. *'Gerhard speech is so boring; his own employees look like they want to strangle themselves.'* My heart sank, my eyes continued down the page. *'Mendelium—choking out the competition'*

James saw where I was looking and turned it off.

"No," he said, "nothing good can come out of that. How about you and I go grab a drink? Call it a late lunch and take the afternoon off?"

I shook my head. His heart was in the right place, but I had no desire to parade myself through the building while people craned their necks and laughed. No, I needed to deal with this the only way I knew how. I needed to pass the time and place these thoughts as far from my head as possible.

"I appreciate it, but I just want to be alone."

He nodded at me, scratching the back of his head, and stood up, "If you need anything at all…. Just let me know alright?"

"I know," I said, "I appreciate you telling me."

He left, closing the door behind him. I stood up and locked it, closing the shades and turning down the lights. I turned off all notifications and cut myself off from the rest of the world. *I couldn't dwell on it.* For too many years I let the laughs affect me. I was who I was because of those tics—the crazy guy jerking his head and pulling on his tie was only a part of my life, but they couldn't see the other part. I might have looked odd in the real world, but in front of this screen I could fly. My computer came alive in front of me.

I delved into Mendelium's codebase, finding a portion in need of improvement. I opened a new branch and began my work. The thoughts of people laughing at my video faded, their insults and mocking glances fell from my thoughts. Instead, my brain was saturated by the code, I moved through it. With it. Each file felt like a section of my psyche, each piece of code mapped to a synapse in my own mind. I let the work consume every part of me. No longer was I at Mendelium Tower, no longer was my consciousness housed in this Tourettic body. I was simply the creator of the code, flowing and moving, constructing new electronic life with every key stroke.

I poured the pain into my work, and it gave back to me. With an empty mind, a peace. Clarity. No longer did the problems of my own life matter, the irregularities of the code were all that held my focus. As I refactored, I felt my own thoughts falling into place, my subconscious righting itself in the background. My own codebase was bugged. This model of my own human genome—Charlie Lamarck, version 1.0—had a glitch in its source code. I wouldn't allow the same to happen with the systems I created.

My fingers ached. My work complete. I looked to the window, the black sky looming to my side, the city and the building changed around me while I was locked in time. Everyone would surely be gone now. I stood up and stepped away from the desk, away from my escape, and reality crashed back in. I grabbed my coat and bag and began to leave, but the emotions overcame me.

There was no more code to distract me, no more excuses to forget about the problems in my life. The emotions were here and ignoring them wasn't an option. It was the same as it always was, no matter what I did I would stand out. No matter how useful I made myself, all I would ever be is different. I broke down in my chair, sobbing to myself in the empty building.

CHAPTER 19

––––––

"It's an exact copy of the previous Template," Gerhard whispered, hand outstretched with a flash drive as he rolled past me in the entry way of Mendelium Tower. "One where Tourette's syndrome still exists. You have twenty minutes. Go."

I connected with his cold green eyes. *No more thinking, no more planning, no more games.* Time to shut up and let my actions speak. I squeezed the drive into my palm and nodded. He continued toward the Template production room, as CEO he got the honors of announcing the production of the Template serum.

I bolted to the elevator, slinging my laptop in a side bag, my shoe falls echoing through the empty back hallways. My pass unlocked each and every door. Past storage closets and back offices I navigated to the service elevator. Just minutes ago, I'd felt lethargic. Gerhard brought about an entirely different side of me. His grit and perseverance were intoxicating, if he wanted something in life, he did it. Maybe I could do the same.

Nineteen minutes.

The elevator doors closed, and I began my rattling ascent towards the roof. I gripped onto the bar and closed my eyes, hoping with my every thought that the elevator wouldn't break down. A single issue or hang up and our plan would fail. *Would that even be so bad?* I was about to break into one of the most interconnected computers in the world. My entire life could collapse around me if the next few minutes went wrong. What terrified me, even more than being caught, was messing up. For a couple hours the backup server would be connected to millions of Template users around the planet. There was no room for mistakes. The elevator rumbled to a halt.

Sixteen minutes.

I scanned my card to open the door. Again, my new position coming in handy. There were no questions when the board director of security wishes to examine the backup servers. The doors opened revealing a room that looked like a miniature version of the server room downstairs. It's minuscule twin, one-hundred stories above.

Fortunately, there were less for security measures than the basement. There was a state-of-the-art door locking system, but no security guard posted up here. Normally there might be more people using the elevator, but the announcement of Template production always drew a large crowd. Gerhard insisted that as much of the company as possible attend, it was his idea to use it as a cover.

There were video cameras on the entrance and strategically pointing at the server. It was challenging to hide from other humans—but I had a way with machines—I would have to cover up my steps carefully. I couldn't waste any time.

I searched around the small area, with barely enough space for me to move around the singular humming machine. The claustrophobic room had concrete walls. Probably a good thing, being this high up would only have served to disorient me. Nearly two thousand feet above the city, the only thing overhead was the rod that emitted the Template signal. Finally, I found a place to connect to the vibrating machine.

Fourteen minutes.

My knees jammed up against the wall as I positioned myself next to the server. We were all alone— the server and me. *Just breathe.* I opened the screen of my laptop, the familiar bright glow reflecting off my glasses.

A part of my brain switched on. The part that I didn't have access to when I navigated the real world. I connected to the system, diving into my terminal, and exploring the computer. Swimming through its files like a shark through a reef. The command line was just a thin veil between my brain and the inner workings of the machine. I saw the file structure and shape of the data through the glowing pixels. Slowly my laptop became like another part of my body—one that didn't tic or spasm against my control—the keyboard just an extension of my physique. This was my world, and I prowled through it with precision.

Ten minutes.

The system was only a grain of sand compared to what lay beneath Mendelium Tower's bottom floor.

Even still it took time to traverse through all the files. This was merely a copy—a backup—designed to take over if there was an error with the monolithic system in the basement. In a few moments that's exactly what would happen. The device I placed would deploy, a bag of water would burst into the tube. This backup system would be the single source of truth for the Template production machine downstairs and the millions of people using it around the world. It was only a temporary measure, but temporary was all we needed, production of the Template serum would finish in a few hours.

I plugged the flash drive into my machine and navigated through the code, feeling around the file structure, observing the code's trends and patterns. Then I switched back into the server. It felt like an ocean compared to the tiny drop of water of data in the flash drive. I found a match.

Six minutes.

The file transfer began. Formatting the data on the drive to the machine in front of me. Smoothing over the rough edges, careful to ensure I didn't leave anything out of place. The percentage bar slowly crept up. A fully sequenced human genome was around 200 gigabytes of data, millions of sets of genomes were stored in our monolithic system in the basement, fortunately for me I simply needed to transfer their new instructions. The procedures that would control future Homo sapiens genetic code. Even still it was a massive amount of data.

There wasn't time to examine every line of the Template. Even if I did it would be too difficult to understand. The codes and languages used to design the Template genome was a task better left to our science department. I had no choice but to trust the data Gerhard gave me would run smoothly. The fan in my machine whirred, the metal of my keyboard growing warm underneath my hands. My computer worked as hard as I did to process all the information. A notification crossed my screen: TRANSFER COMPLETED.

Four minutes.

I breathed out a sign of relief, but my work wasn't yet through. When the police investigate a crime, they analyze every possible action and motivation of the offender. Checking for fingerprints in the physical world and monitoring all activity of mobile devices in the surrounding area. The digital world was no different. Every keystroke I typed into the machine was like a fingerprint, all trackable and traceable by those keen enough to know what to look for. But I was a step ahead. I understood their security protocols, anticipating each of their tools to track and retain data about me. I was like an electronic mirage—here one minute, nonexistent in the next.

Two minutes.

Sweat grew at my brow, my heart may have been racing in my chest. I was the flashing cursor in front of me. I was the code that flowed out of my fingertips and into the server. I bounced around the file structure, gracefully navigating and searching across its every corner. I found video surveillance, removing all footage from this room in the last hours. I located the elevator logs, deleting any trace I'd moved around the building. Adding functions to cover up my return trip back downstairs. The ideas flowed into my mind like I was a conduit to another realm. I created new scripts to obscure all activity that could implicate Gerhard and myself, leaving the new Template outline perfectly poised in the process. The pressure polished my thinking, the rush refined my skill.

One minute.

I flew through the server now. Riding through the directories and modules using my command line. The ideas, concerns, and worries stopped. There were no more tracks to cover, no more data to manipulate and hide. I looked to the clock one more time, disconnecting my laptop from the machine.

Zero.

I stood up; my knees relieved from being jammed into the small space. It was done. Right then another notification came through to my screen:

DEPLOYMENT SUCCESSFUL.

I closed my laptop and walked out of the room. Right this second the bag of water would deploy, forcing the servers to reroute everything to the backup computer upstairs. Each step brought a sense of accomplishment, my breathing excited and calm all at once. I stepped into the elevator, slowly descending through the company I'd just undermined. I smiled, not because I was successful, but because there was no more doubts or indecision filling my mind. I did it.

CHAPTER 20

———

We walked through into the ballroom; Liz's arm attached to mine. Her flowing green dress moved like it was an extension of her body. I wore a black suit, and a forest green tie to match her, each of my movements felt awkward in comparison to the poise of hers. Mendelium Tower was a different world tonight, the ballroom transformed, tapestries hung down either side of the entrance accentuating yellow light from the room beyond. We walked through the archway and into another realm, it was the same room I'd been in many times before, but the space felt alive. The smells of appetizers wafted from near the bar, the soft sound of music wrapping around us.

"See anyone you know?" I asked Liz.

"You're the one that works here," she said as she looked around the room. She wore a gold necklace and her hair up, I admired her for a moment, quickly looking away as her eyes came to mine.

"Well," I said.

She smirked, "Yes, I do see some friends."

James stood near the bar, wrapped up in a deep conversation with another member of the board. He wore his standard, perfectly fitted, grey suit with a glass of dark brown alcohol in hand. I wanted to speak with him, so much had happened in my life in these last couple weeks, but I feared I wouldn't get the chance. Tonight, was a night to celebrate, but I had other plans.

"When do you think you'll sneak away," Liz whispered to me, the smell of her perfume touching my nose as she leaned in close.

"I'm going to wait until the celebration begins, the more people are distracted the better."

"Just promise me you'll be safe."

I nodded back at her. *Why had it taken me so long to tell her?* Having Liz on board made everything in life simple. It was her idea to sneak away during the party tonight. Brilliant, as usual. It gave me an excuse to sneak around the rest of the building with no-one else around to see me.

"Let's find our seats," I said and began walking through the crowd. There were still those who looked at me with judgmental eyes, but my new position on the board generated more fake smiles and handshakes than before.

We walked past the place Dave died. People stood there conversing, oblivious to what happened there a month before. Liz glanced at me while we walked past, a remorseful look on her face. There were fewer police officers around the building lately, the investigation must have come to a halt. I looked down on the spot, just as I had on that night, it was hard to believe how much a single moment changed the trajectory of my life. Things felt like they were going so well now, should I have felt guilty that my own fortune was due to another's death?

"It looks like we have a visitor," Liz said, a smile brightening her face. I expected one the board members, but instead I saw a small yellow dress and a ponytail.

"Grace," Liz said, sitting at the table next to her in the spot assigned to me. "I didn't know you were going to be here. Where is your dad?"

"He's getting ready; he says it's best for him to be alone before speaking in front of people."

"So, what are you going to do?" Liz asked.

"Dad has a table for me up front, he promised there would be really good food here tonight."

"As good as yours?" I asked.

"Not a chance," she said with a grin, still looking down at the pictures in front of her.

"What do you have there?" Liz asked.

"Some bird pictures I drew, I told you I would show them to you," she moved aside the partially finished one she had been working on and pulled out another. A blue bird, with an attention to detail I didn't know was possible from a child. Its cornflower blue head and wings looked animated on the page; it was in full flight gliding across a forested background. I could even visualize the wind underneath the bird's wings.

"This is incredible," Liz said, sounding as shocked as I felt.

"I love bluebirds," she said, "they were always Mom's favorite. She used to sit outside near the garden and watch them in the morning."

Liz met my eyes again for a moment, I couldn't quite read her expression. There was a layer of sadness for Grace, but something else I couldn't place.

"I like the males the best," she continued, "the red-orange on their breast and the blues are brighter than on the females."

"How many of these drawing do you have?" I asked.

"A bunch, do you want to see them?"

"Absolutely," I said, taking the seat on the other side of her.

"I told Dad that you two would like them," she pulled out more. Each of them with as much detail as the first. She showed us many of them, each time her face lighting up, excited to share with us the details and facts about each one.

"Good evening," Gerhard said, his booming voice cutting over the music. My coworkers began to fill the seats in front of us.

"Hey Grace," I said, standing up, "I have to go, do you think you can keep Liz occupied while I'm gone?"

She nodded back at me as her father continued to speak from the front of the room.

"This is the largest production of the Template Mendelium has ever produced. I want to thank everyone involved in the process; our team has been put through more stress over these last few weeks than I would have wished. But we've done something incredible. We must never lose sight of what we are doing for the world, eliminating disease one child at a time."

I tried not to roll my eyes as he laid on the world-changing ideas a little too thick. We saw eye to eye on some things, but in this area, we couldn't have been more different. He was willing to go in front of all these people, while behind everyone's back scheme to do the opposite. People respected his opinion, why couldn't he just speak the truth?

Being far away allowed me to examine him in a way I couldn't across a desk. His large smile, not a hair out of place with a part that looked decided upon by a public relations team. It amazed me how put together he was for a man missing so many body parts, even sitting in a chair he seemed to tower over the room. *I wish we could have done this another way.*

I snuck out the door, against the current of the crowd pushing into the room. I didn't need stealth, I didn't need a team, planning a world-shaking failure at Mendelium took only a few hours of planning and the right levels of access. I first went up to my office, grabbing the box of test run Template's. I put on the confident air of my new title and set off towards the production room.

I smiled looking up at the security camera. I'd programmed a convenient script to deal with them. Using recorded data of me across the internet to recognize my facial features, replacing all segments of me walking through Mendelium Tower with a video loop taken immediately before

My watch ticked while I rounded another downward flight of stairs. Time wasn't as tight as it was at the server room, but I still had to avoid running into anyone. *What if I did get caught?* I'd rehearsed excuses, but they wouldn't matter if someone saw me. I pursued this career for the sake of creating a family, to build a life we loved together, but my actions tonight didn't align with this story I kept telling myself. It still felt right. Every logical part of me argued against it, but I felt alive, I had an opportunity to do something real.

I left the stairwell arriving on the bottom floor of Mendelium Tower, my shoes clacked on the polished granite. With half of the lights turned off it looked more ominous than it had earlier in the day. There were always some workers in the building, but my odds of running into one tonight were near zero with the party happening.

Get in and get out. The individual actions aren't going to be difficult but the plan itself caused anxiety to bubble beneath my sternum. Before long I was down the hallway and standing in front of the entrance to the production room. The cameras pointed at the door. I stepped through, trusting in the ability of my code to foil the surveillance system.

I walked through the rows of Templates that had just finished production. Carrying my chest high I strode ahead, the decision was made, there was no more time to worry. The sprawling room was empty, even with the dim lighting it was difficult to see all the way across. I weaved through the rows, millions of vials of Template serum covering the tables. Retracing my steps, I found the storage room again walking straight to the locked cupboard, I extended the key card, closing my eyes and desperately hoping for a green light. It came, flashing for a moment and illuminating my hands in front of me. I expected them to be shaking but they held steady. There was no blinking or jitters tonight. I pulled the doors open and saw all the scanners lining the cupboard. My plan was sound. Time to work.

Rewriting the software of the scanners would have been fascinating, but sometimes in programming the simplest answers are the best ones. Why make life harder than it had to be? Some problems are so complex that it's better to go around them completely. I grabbed the first scanner and opened the box I'd brought down from my office. Pulling out a screwdriver I took off the back of the scanner exposing the motherboard and wiring connected to it.

Figuring out what to do was easy when I had a test scanner at home. As much as our team liked to think we had the highest level of security it didn't take me long to find a way around. I dug through the code, letting my mind work. The more I read, the more it began to shape an image in my subconscious. With every file I passed through a picture came into focus. An outsider saw words and symbols, but to my practiced mind, a tapestry formed. I could *feel* the way the data flowed in and out of the system. Understanding precisely what code triggered when the scanner turned on, and what would happen when the scanner failed.

Then I knew.

The vials attached to the scanner, detecting if the nutrient levels of each liquid matched up with the Template. After the switch every single one of them would pass the scan. It wasn't enough just to change the Template, we had to make sure no one noticed.

In programming everything is built upon binary code. Zeros and ones. True or false. The code for the scanner was no different, it used programming languages that I was unfamiliar with, but at the core they all worked on the same principles. The code checked that the serum levels matched the Template, if they did it would show a success, if not a failure. So, I switched it. What was once a zero was now a one.

Every time the scanner examined a Template that didn't match the expected output it would succeed rather than fail. Gerhard's plan to do a test run was brilliant, allowing me to practice with a Template and a scanner in the comfort of my own home.

I added my code to the first scanner with ease. Grabbing the second, then the third, growing faster with each one. It was so simple it almost seemed too easy. I finished, leaving the storage closet, the last of my work complete. Lingering on the glimmering vials across the expanse of tables.

If someone ever found out what we'd done I'd seem insane. It felt so obvious to me that Tourette's syndrome's existence made the world a better place. I'd always hoped that when I became a father one of my children would share those genes with me. The syndrome defined my entire existence. Who wouldn't want to share such a big part of their life with their child?

The only thing that made me nervous was circumnavigating the standard quality assurance process. If something went wrong with one of these vials I would be to blame. Defects were unlikely. A fraction of a percent—but these weren't just numbers. They were people's lives. Children who would grow up dealing with the repercussions of my decisions. I put the thought from my mind. *Nothing would go wrong.*

I had no idea how much time had passed, everything went smoothly, but the pressure of the night caused time to move at a glacial pace. I didn't check my watch, it didn't matter. I needed to get back to the party before dinner finished. I flew past the rows of vials, feeling the warmth of accomplishment.

My footsteps echoed again as I cruised through the thin hallway to the production floor. I passed through two sets of doors; each time relieved I hadn't run into anyone else requiring me to make excuses for why I was walking around the production room at night. I passed through a back hallway, disposing the box of used Templates and spare parts in a waste basket. Any anxiety melted as I left the last trace of my digressions behind me. I exited the hallway into the main entry-way of Mendelium Tower, this late in the evening all the windows where dark, the cold fluorescent light above glowed off of the freshly polished granite.

I walked towards the main stairwell, planning to sneak back into the party unseen. No one would know the difference. I stopped. Two men crossed the large floor walking directly towards me, their badges flashed as they passed beneath the lights.

For a moment I thought I should run, I was so close to the door, so close to freedom. It was too late, the damage was done.

"Good evening Mr. Lamarck, enjoying yourself on an evening stroll?" Said the shorter one with a slight hobble in his step.

"...Yes?"

"I'm Bill Taylor" he said, "and this is my partner, Mike Guerrera." he said gesturing to the younger man with dark slicked back hair and dull brown eyes examining me. "We are going to need you to come with us."

CHAPTER 21

FIVE YEARS EARLIER

I walked down the concrete sidewalks. Carefully balancing the hot coffee in my hand as I moved with the crowds and traffic. I smelled my cup. Not daring to drink the scalding liquid while I walked. These days I didn't even feel like I needed it. Even at 5 o'clock in the morning, before the sun's rays peered through the buildings, my steps were fast, and my brain was ready to start the day. The commuters around me looked tired, their faces locked forward, each set of eyes as cold and dead as the next. I felt a little bit guilty as I hopped across another sidewalk, I loved what I did and couldn't wait to get to work.

I was careful not to hold the coffee too close to me, not wanting to spill a drop on my baggy sweatshirt. For a while I attempted to dress the part of my new position, to look more responsible and older than I truly was. I'd grown out my beard and cut my hair short, I even started wearing a suit jacket. But it just didn't feel like *me*. On days like this I was more than happy to be clean shaven and wear an unassuming grey sweatshirt. It didn't make any real sense, but those stiff business costumes always made my code feel less artistic. I didn't feel like myself when I wore them, and the code could tell. When people came looking for me, coworkers would tell them to look for the homeless guy in the director's office.

The only thing that matters is the work—Director of Technology at GeniSense. I always said the title didn't mean anything, but damn did it feel good coming out of my mouth. All those moments of self-doubt when I was younger, the insults people would fling at me, they didn't matter now. I'd risen above them, attaining a level of success I hadn't thought possible. I was just a weird twitchy kid, that self-image never seemed to go away no matter how much money I spent on my clothes or paid to a barber.

I waited at another crosswalk. I ticced, my head jolting to the side, my right hand spasming, it didn't bother me. No longer was I surrounded by people who enjoyed pointing out my differences, I'd found a new family of my own. I'd thrown my entire life into my work. Into the code and into the people—and it gave back to me. Rather than being ostracized for my differences, people cared about my ideas. We programmers are a strange bunch, unconcerned with how charming someone's smile was, what really mattered was the code. And when it came to the code no one could compete. I could only do one thing well in life, but that skill brought with it so much prosperity. It brought money, it brought friends, but more importantly it brought meaning to my life. The way I contributed to the world improved my coworkers' lives, and hopefully, the lives of others.

I passed under some scaffolding, through the poor parts of the city, our offices were far from the giant buildings like Mendelium Tower. I always wondered what it might be like there, at the pinnacle of genetic technology, but in this moment, I was satisfied with the important work I did in our own corner of the world.

Break-ins and vandalism weren't uncommon in the east district, it was the up-and-coming area of the city, I liked to think being in the heart of downtown breathed a certain kind of life into our company. We couldn't get too complacent seeing the lower castes of society struggling at our doorstep. At the same time, I didn't want to put anyone in danger. Hopefully hiring Li would help with that, a security guard at our entrance should make everyone feel more comfortable. Especially one so welcoming and kind. Li already felt like the kind grandfather of GeniSense, unfortunately I would get into the office before him this morning and miss his warm welcome.

Our street was still dark despite the traffic lights blurring past me, in one of those flashes I noticed glass on the ground. It wasn't uncommon for graffiti on the side of our building now and then, but there had never been a break in before. I walked up to the side of the building, the bricks light brown, the color wasn't drastically different from the sea of grey and blacks downtown, but it felt unique. The buildings here had more shape, more character. Sure enough, the window was broken in. I placed my keys in the door cautiously, quietly turning the key and door-knob. Someone likely threw a brick through the window. *But a brick wouldn't have made that big a hole.*

I ticced. Head snapping to the side again and my right hand spasming near my pocket. I was just their passenger, at least until I sat down in front of the screen. The back room was dark. I loved to arrive this early in the morning for many reasons, but the silent stillness echoing through GeniSense's offices was not one of them. I shouldn't be concerned; we have a fully functional security system. If someone broke into the building, there would be alarms going off right now. The beautiful wooden floors were just one of the many characteristics I enjoyed about work-ing in the older districts of the city, but the creaks and groans as I moved through the building were not.

I came to the light switch flicking it on. The room around me looked untouched save for the glass shat-tered across the table beneath the window, some of the papers strewn across the floor. *Likely just a gust from the window.* I flipped another panel of switches, illuminating the adjacent offices and the hallway. I continued, down the narrow hallway, approaching another door. I moved slowly, listening intently as I looked around the office. Everything here looked untouched. I took a sip of my coffee and walked towards the front entrance. Cars and pedestrians continued walking by in front of the large glass pane. I ticced, arm contorting by my side. I came to the main panel of switches at the front, the ones that controlled the lights for the entire building. One by one I switched them. Lights came on the storefront, and lights would slowly be coming on in the offices upstairs. I sat down my bag.

Footsteps. Someone moving on the floor above me, I must have spooked them by turning on the power. The wood groaned and creaked above me, it sounded like multiple pairs of feet shuffling across the floor.

I froze. Coffee in my left hand and bag still hanging at my side. I backed away from the staircase and closer to the main entrance. Back across broken glass. Should I just leave? Whoever they were it wasn't worth getting hurt—

"Stop, put your hands in the air."

I spun, my eyes wide, a few police officers fumbled with the door behind me. My eyes didn't stay wide for long, the tics came on alongside the stress. I tried desperately to hold them in. My eyelids slammed shut, blacking out my world like an inverse strobe light, my arm jolting by my side.

"Place your hands over your head," said the cop nearest to the front. His eyes scanned the room, he looked calm, but his right hand was resting near his belt. My rapid tics set him on edge, I would have to hold them in.

"I… I just got here… this wasn't me," I said through panicked breath. The caffeine from the coffee coming up right alongside the flush of adrenaline. He cautiously stepped closer to me, scanning my face, looking for any sign of something off. I still heard some noises upstairs, but the two officers focused only on me.

"Are we cool?" He asked me, his voice got lower and his left-hand gesturing for his buddies to hold back. I could see their postures stiffen.

"Yes," I shouted, my tics mounting, I tried everything in my power to keep them in.

"Are you tweaking on something son?"

"No, no, this is just the way I am," I began, but the tics couldn't be held down any longer. The erupted from me completely outside of my control. "I have Touret—"

I didn't finish my sentence. My feet left the ground, the officer's shoulder smashing down into my ribs as we landed. Something inside my chest popped. The hot coffee fell to the floor behind me, burning the skin on my arm.

I realized my mistake as it was happening, my arm jolted involuntarily next to my pocket. He thought I was a tweaker grabbing for a weapon.

The weight came in and I felt like I was drowning. I writhed in pain beneath the officer, laying in the scalding coffee and pinned to the ground.

CHAPTER 22

———

I sat with my arms crossed at a metal table. Each time I rested my hands down I pulled them back up, it was freezing. *Was their goal to make me uncomfortable?* The situation alone was enough for that. I felt down to my ribs, remembering my last encounter with the police. A past life, I was barely the same person today. Hopefully this version of me could perform better than the last, what I said in these next moments would be critical.

After their introduction, Bill and Mike took me to at room on the seventeenth floor of Mendelium Tower. It looked like it used to be a large storage closet, but it had been transformed into a makeshift interrogation room. There were no windows, just a single blinding light hanging above.

The door swung open, hitting against the back wall. The loud noise might have shocked me, but I was already on red alert.

"Well Mr. Lamarck" Bill said casually, "you want to explain to us why you were wondering around so far away from the party? We've been meaning to interview you from some time. Seeing you out of your seat during Gerhard's speech gave us pause, care to tell us what you were up to?"

"You can call me Charlie," I said. "And I'm not particularly fond of the parties. Or large gatherings of people in general for that matter, I wanted to take a walk around the building to set my mind at ease."

"That tracks," Bill said to Mike as he sat down across from me. Mike's hair looked like it contained half a bottle of hair gel as it shined beneath the bright overhead light. *Did they bring in their own lighting?* Mendelium's lights didn't bear into my eyes, not like this one did.

"How about you start by telling us about your relationship with Dave?" he asked.

"I only knew him a little, we weren't close."

Bill nodded along; Mike's glare was as cold as the table.

"So, the two of you didn't spend time together outside of work?"

"Not at all," I said, my blinking getting rapid again. *Shit.* Stressing about not looking guilty was causing me to have facial tics.

"Were you aware of Dave's propensity to…" Bill paused briefly and looked at Mike, "mix business with pleasure?"

"What exactly do you mean by that?"

"I think you know damn well what we mean by that," Bill said.

"He did enjoy parties," I said. If they were trying to loosen me up to say more about what I was doing down in production this wasn't the way to do it. *Had they been watching me?* "He did quality work, but I always tried to keep my distance, the two of us never got along. He loved to wine and dine our wealthy partners. It involved a lot more wining than dining."

Mike shared a look with Bill, "We were referring to his relations with his... female coworkers."

"Ah..." I said, "He told his wife and kids he was working late a lot; he sure wasn't working with me."

"Did his wife know?" Bill asked.

I sighed, thinking about the last time I'd seen his wife Cynthia and their kids during the speech Gerhard gave. It was so easy for me to resent the man, to forget the void and sadness he left behind, "I don't think she did, there is no way she would have put up with him if she had figured any of it out. I have to say, I really don't think I'm the best person to ask about all of this."

"Do you think he deserved her?" Bill asked.

"I hadn't thought about it like that—no. I don't understand why any of this matters. Dave was a bad husband, a bad father, and in my opinion a bad person—but he was talented. I have opinions about his personal life, but that was Dave."

I blinked five times in quick succession.

"How have—"

I blinked rapidly again in another burst. Like a sneeze erupting, I'd held them in too long. The floodgates opened, the battle against my physical body lost.

"Are you alright?" Mike asked.

"I'm fine," I shot back. "It's been a long couple of weeks, we've been in such a rush at work, and I still don't feel comfortable with my place on the board." I took off my glasses and set them on the table, rubbing my hands over my eyes. Pushing in, wishing I could pin the eyelids down and my face could function like a normal person's for a few minutes.

"How have things changed for you at work since his death?" Mike asked uncrossing his arms.

"Stressful." I stated, "I had a good thing going before, I got to focus on work I was good at. I understand why the board chose me, I have the expertise, but programming was always my specialty, not public speaking or meetings. Each passing day is a reminder of why I'm not right for the job."

"No," said Bill, "you don't exactly seem like the charming type."

"Sure doesn't," Mike agreed.

"Board member though… that's a prestigious position," Bill stated.

"I suppose," I said putting my glasses back on.

"You don't agree?"

"No, it is…" I said, giving into another barrage of blinks.

Bill relaxed, "Do you know why we pulled you in here tonight?"

I shook my head.

"We suspect Dave's death was not an accident."

Being scrutinized so closely made me feel the need to exaggerate my emotions, hopefully counteract my tics a bit. I nodded, and attempted to hide the relief I felt, they didn't seem like they had any idea what I'd been up to mere minutes ago.

"We found some drugs in Dave's system," Bill said.

"That's nothing out of the ordinary," I said, "I think that would have been true most weekends in the last few years."

"We did find a handful of things in his system. Cocaine, ecstasy...." Bill started.

"We don't need to give him every small detail," Mike said, cutting him off. "Can you think of any reason someone would want Dave dead?"

I took a moment, recognizing how closely these two were watching me, worried they were analyzing every little emotional response. Did they look for surprise in my face? It didn't come as one, the police had been all over Mendelium Tower since Dave's death. *How guilty did twitching make me look?*

"That's why I'm here? You think I'm a suspect?"

The two men looked at me blankly, amusement growing on Bill's face.

"This has made my life a living hell," I said, "Do you think I wanted to sacrifice a job I enjoyed for *this*? The constant stress? The fights with my wife? I didn't have a choice, no one even asked me. And for what? For a company full of people who don't even respect my opinions."

They both stared back for a minute before Bill broke the silence, "Well you certainly don't seem to be handing it well."

The beginning of a headache pulsed against my temples, I had another Tourettic outburst, my eye muscles now exhausted from the uncontrolled spasms.

"No, I didn't like the man, but I could have called the police about his drug usage if I really wanted him out of my life."

"Do you know anyone else with a reason to harm Dave?" Mike asked.

"I don't," I said, "are you insinuating it might be a murder?"

"Afraid we can't tell you that," Bill grumbled.

"I can't imagine anyone at Mendelium having something to gain. It's been stressful on everyone, especially this close to the Template production. He had a lot of connections though, an entire other life, maybe he got in deep with some dangerous people."

"Sure," Bill said slowly.

"Do you need anything else from me? This week has been long as hell and I was supposed to be out with my wife."

"Actually, we do have one final question for you," Bill began, "we recently came across a video. One that doesn't portray you in the best light, are you aware of the video in question?"

"Of course."

"What do you know about it?" He asked.

"What do I *know* about it? I know that it was fucking humiliating. I know that it's something I actively try to avoid thinking about. It made my life hell."

"I apologize," he said, pausing for a moment to see if I had more to say.

I didn't.

"Were you aware that Dave was one of the first people to post the video?"

I shook my head.

Bill nodded, as Mike looked on from the back of the room.

"I had no idea," I said, the two of them examined my emotions. I felt a flush of rage towards Dave, followed by a short moment of gratitude for his death. Any attempt to hide my emotions failed. I could only hope they sensed my genuine surprise. "That video has haunted me. I would have done nearly anything to take it down, but I had no idea he was involved."

"Thank you for answering all of our question Charlie," Mike said.

"You're welcome, can I get back to my wife now?"

"Sure Charlie," Bill smiled, "we'll be keeping in touch, if you learn anything else, please let us know immediately."

Mike gave a weak smile and opened the door for me. I tried not to leap through it and run straight out of there. I was busy thanking any kind of deity or fate that allowed me to slip through this night unscathed. Dave's death was the furthest thing from my mind, a part of me was curious what had happened, but right now my freedom was too sweet to taste anything else.

I walked alone through Mendelium Tower, back towards the maintenance area, past the smells of the kitchen that lingered in the air. The party would be over by now. I wonder if Liz was worried about me, I'd been gone much longer than I'd expected.

I was successful. Everything we'd been working for, all the stress and nights spent lying awake had paid off. I now had time. *We* now had time, Gerhard and I had more work in front of us, but at least we'd given our-selves a chance. I'd now put so much faith in the man. His word being the only thing I had moving forward. *What else did he have planned?* There was so much behind those calculating eyes. I now had to place my faith in him, there was simply nothing else I could do.

I straightened my suit jacket again as I walked past some party guests, people funneled out the door. The last stragglers, grabbing their jackets and talking to their dates. The lowlights of the party now bright, the serving and banquet staff cleaned off the tables and reorganized the room. I walked up to one of the servers, she was grabbing empty wine glasses off the table.

"Excuse me," I said, "I'm looking for my wife, I think she might still be around here. Braided blonde hair, with a flowing green dress? Have you seen her anywhere?"

She just shook her head at me, as I looked around the room. There was no one left here, but I couldn't imagine she would leave without me.

"Hey," said a young bus boy, his scrawny arms carrying a big stack of plates. "I think she's back in the kitchen."

"Really?"

"I saw a woman who looked just like that," he said. "She was with her daughter; I just saw them a minute ago."

"Thanks," I said, walking towards the back of the room. I exited through the staff door at the back of the room. Through the tiled kitchen hallways, following the smell of cooking food.

"There he is," Gerhard said. His chair perched off to the side of the grill. He looked out of place back here in the kitchens, the air of authority he carried and his expensive suit looked strange next to the garbage can and freezer.

"Hey Charlie," Liz said from behind the grill, next to her Grace was diligently stirring something on the stovetop. "Grace is teaching me a few things."

"She's not learning very fast," Grace said as she watched the simmering pot intently.

"She tells me she can make a better risotto than what was served at dinner tonight," Liz said.

"I can," she said confidently, "they overcooked it, and they didn't even use Arborio rice."

"Why don't you join me," Gerhard said, gesturing to a chair at his side. I sat, watching the two of them work together. Grace laser focused on the task at hand as Liz looked at her fondly. She did seem comfortable with her, she brought out a different side of Liz I didn't get to see that often, a side I loved.

"How did things go?" He asked, lowering his voice as Grace explained how much olive oil she used to Liz.

"It's done. I ran into two officers on my way back, they pulled me into a room for questioning."

The comfortable smile fell from his face. "Tonight? I specifically asked for them not to bother employees during the party. I'm sorry Charlie. What did they ask you?"

"Nothing related to the Template, but a few questions about Dave. Apparently, I'm one of the people who has gained the most from his passing. Why is this investigation continuing?"

For a moment he looked frustrated, taking his eyes off Grace and Liz, "I wish I could give you the answer Charlie, but they've demanded full access to the staff. Were you able to fix all of the scanners without being seen?"

I nodded. Liz looked up from Grace towards Gerhard and me, her soft smiling eyes meeting mine. All this selfishness could finally end, she was as stressed about this as I was. She just took on my problems in stride, gladly helping me along the way.

"We might just be able to do this Charlie. Human-kind stands at a turning point, you and I are going to play a role in its future. I think this calls for a celebration. His chair moved in front of me, back into the kitchen, returning with two glasses and a bottle of bourbon.

"Will you indulge me?" He asked.

"I would be honored. We did it."

He splashed the brown alcohol in each glass, and we clinked them together. Sipping on it in unison and watching the two most important women in each of our lives laugh together behind the stove. It was done. This phase of my life, as stressful and brief as it had been, was finally over. I felt a brief surge of fulfillment, but something else was there too. I looked around the kitchen, to my wife and Grace, to Gerhard, looking content and sipping on a drink. This chapter would now come to a close, I wasn't sure if I was ready for it to end. I put the glass to my lips, taking a sip, attempting to savor every second.

CHAPTER 23

————

R ain pattered against my office window as I focused on the screen in front of me. Perched above the rest of the city, the glass walls of Mendelium Tower were beautiful on clear days, but storms like this one it affected the entire mood of the office. The residual light that funneled through the building was gone; the rain drops echoed through the floor masking all other sounds. It was perfect. All day long people on our floor complained about the weather, and all day long I smiled to myself and ignored them. The low light and white noise of the rain cut off the rest of the world. No more sounds of water cooler conversations, no more traffic noise or movement from the city below.

I sat with the code, my fingers dancing across the keyboard. The concepts and ideas dissolved, beneath it a layer of pure artistic creativity. My mind bended the will of the machine, creating commands and rules, hopping between different files in the code-base. Moments like this didn't come often anymore, it needed to be cherished. Time fell away like the water against my office window.

"You're still here," James, said walking into my office, our floor empty except for a few fellow workaholics.

I looked up at him. Blinking rapidly, as my eyes adjusted from the computer. Only a few seconds away from the code and the tics came right back.

I smiled at him, but immediately noticed something off. He didn't carry himself in the way he normally did.

"Are you alright?" I asked, noting the sweat marks developing in the armpits of his red button up, his jaw clenched.

"I'm not sure," he said, taking a seat, and shifting around in it. I waited for him to start chatting with me, but he never did. He just sat.

"Well?" I asked, more sternly than I meant to, he clearly wasn't himself.

"It's been a long few days," he said, voice thin compared to the booming confidence he normally brought along with him. He smiled, but there was a strain behind it I hadn't noticed before. "Have you spoke to the detectives yet?"

I nodded, "The night of the party, they took me up to the seventh floor and questioned me about Dave."

"I was just down there."

"And?"

"I don't know, I'm concerned they know a lot more than they're letting on."

"Did they accuse you of something?" I asked.

"No, nothing like that, but I'm worried Charlie. Did they ask to see you and Liz's house?"

I shook my head again. His mouth twisted and he stood up, "I would say I have nothing to hide, but we both know that's not true."

He looked back over this shoulder and through the door. I don't think I'd ever seen him this nervous. I never even stopped to think about him with the investigation. I thought only of what might happen to me if our plan failed, James had just as much to lose. If the officers questioned people across Mendelium, they might learn about James's dealing. I sat there for a moment watching him stress, feeling like a terrible friend. How many times had he dropped what he was doing to help me relax?

"James wait," I said as he turned to leave. "I'm sure that it'll be all right, their investigation has nothing at all to do with you. If people admit to using substances you've sold them, they would be putting themselves into trouble as well. There is no reason this investigation should turn up anything on you."

"That's true," he said, flashing a smile, but looking down at the floor.

"You shouldn't have to worry, he wasn't one of your clients, no one would think you supplied whatever cocktail of substances he was on when he died."

"No, of course not," he said, still not meeting my eyes.

"I'm not sure how you normally do this, you've been so supportive to me in the past. You've been there for me time and time again. How can I help? Tell me what I can do."

He gave me a frustrated stare, "I appreciate it C, I do, but I don't think I'm going to be able to think straight unless I get some things in order."

He gave me a head nod, then left. What the *hell*. I've never seen him like this, a shell of the James I knew. I should have been more understanding, there must have been some way I could have helped him. Every time when I needed someone, he was there for me. I started to go after him, but looking around the floor, he was already gone.

I sat back down to my desk and my gaze drifted out over the city, my head swimming in more thoughts than before. The dreary weather echoed my mood. Our plan was in motion. Another generation of Tourette's syndrome would begin soon. *Should I feel more guilty?* I changed the lives of children that hadn't been born yet, I made a decision impacting thousands of lives. What if I was wrong?

For a small percentage of people, it would shape their world forever, something they could never change or take back. I remembered how much I hated the tics in my youth. Today I recognized how much positivity Tourette's syndrome brought into my life, it was the reason I was so successful at writing code, bringing about elevated focus and creativity. But in the early days I resented myself, would the future generations see it in the same way I did? I couldn't dwell on it. The decision had been made, it was time to live with the consequences of my actions, I pushed it from my mind.

Maybe it was the image of the waterlogged city below me, or the thoughts racing through my head, but I left my office headed straight for Gerhard's. I knew he was in. The look in Anthony's eyes told me the same. "What do you want this time?" He asked using a sharp tone still looking at his monitor.

"I would like to meet with Gerhard." *Why the hell else would I be here.* "How soon will he be available?"

"Currently meeting with an ambassador, followed by some members of our marketing team."

"He has a lot of those lately."

No reply. His finger moved down the page and I saw the screen scrolling from the reflection in his glasses. He made no attempt to interact with me, growing colder with each interaction.

"When will he wrap up?" I asked for a second time.

"He has these meetings scheduled well into the evening."

"Can you let him know I'll be waiting for him?"

"Will it make any difference?" Anthony asked, taking his eyes off the screen, and looking at me. He flashed a white smile, but there was venom behind it. I stared back at him, ignoring his question. "You're going to stay and wait no matter what I say aren't you?"

He may have disliked me, but at least we were beginning to understand each other. I nodded and took a seat in the small reception area, then stared out over the rain clouds from a higher angle.

"Charlie," Gerhard barked as soon as the door to his office slammed shut. "You can't be up here visiting me all the time; it could look suspicious." He looked tired when he greeted me in the hall, his normally perfectly parted hair looked as though he had been running his hand through it and the top button on his shirt sat undone.

"You think Anthony is going to start gossiping about us?" I said sarcastically.

He shot me a glare and didn't respond right away. Gerhard dodged through the obstacles of his office in his wheelchair. I followed almost tripping over the couch while I observed him.

"No, I trust Tony completely. What is it you need?" He calmed his voice and gestured for me to take a seat on his couch.

I sat down to the side of him, looking into the fireplace, now burned down to coals.

"What happens now?" I asked.

"Things are in play; all *you* have to do is wait."

It wasn't just his hair that seemed out of place, there were bags beneath his eyes. His skin even seemed more hollow than usual, though it could have been the low light of the office. He leaned lower in his chair, his presence not commanding the room as it normally did.

"I mean... How do you think people are going to react? Are you going to claim there was some kind of defect with the Template? What about the next round? People are going to resent you. The blowback, if not handled tactfully, could destroy Mendelium forever. What good is changing a single Template if we don't follow through and explain why?"

He smiled at me, "I see I'm not the only one who's been having a rough day."

I narrowed my eyes at him, "How do we intend to deal with the consequences from this? We've been so focused on the first part of our plan that the second has been neglected. In one way, things are finished, but in another, it's just beginning. Your life could change completely when people find out what we did. What if an angry parent tries to retaliate, what about Grace? You could be putting her in danger as well."

All emotions left his face, "I appreciate your concern Charlie, as endearing as I find it, these are the burdens I've chosen to undertake. I gave you my word and I have a plan. You're going to have to trust me."

"Why do I have to trust *you*?" I asked, sitting up. "Don't I deserve to know? I have made myself complicit in this, do you realize how much danger I've put myself into, how much I've sacrificed?"

"Quite frankly Charlie, you have to trust me because you have no say in the matter. You have played your part and now I will play mine—you will be involved no more."

"Are we done? Just like that?" Just days ago, we'd celebrated together, this looked like a completely different man in front of me. *Why go through all of that if his plan was simply to throw me to the curb when he was finished with me?*

"Yes, for now, I think it is for the best. I have a great deal of things to get in place before then, and I can't have you coming in here whenever you please."

I stared blankly at him, I thought we'd built a rapport. Did I misread him? There was no way, the time Liz and I had spent with him and Grace, I saw a life in him then I didn't now.

"I appreciate everything you have done. I owe you so much and I promise we will have much more to discuss once this is over," There was a flash of sadness in his eyes.

"You should take some time away from here Charlie. Spend some time with Liz, I'm sure the two of you could use—"

"You don't know what Liz and I need," I shot back.

"Take a few days off, I'm serious, you look like you could use them."

"I want to help you Gerhard. This was *my* plan; I can help you in put a speech together at least."

"No," Gerhard said, more firmly than before. "We're done, and you *will* be taking a few days away, this is no longer negotiable. I'm putting in a vacation for you, and you *will* take it."

I didn't dare say anything else. Every interjection I'd had moved me backward, I heard the verdict and I would do as the judge commanded.

CHAPTER 24

———

TWO YEARS EARLIER

We got off the plane, spirits high and the evening air warm. Elizabeth and Charlie Lamarck, so far from the coffee shop. It was official, it was time to relax. *But could I?* The stress of the wedding was past, the worries about ticcing in front of an entire crowd behind me. Every time I looked at the camera I imagined one day our children watching their father sporadically snapping his head to one side on his wedding day. My convulsions, documented for eternity.

There was nothing else to worry about, I felt it throughout every muscle in my body, but the feeling never made its way up to my brain. It didn't matter if the tics were around, my body may have stopped spasming, but the thoughts never did. Intrusively tugging at me at every possible opportunity. I couldn't control them, but at least I could point them towards something constructive. There was nothing productive to do on the beach in the sunshine. In my mind I'd looked forward to this, the *idea* of relaxation was bliss. The view of oceans and alcoholic beverages floated into my mind for months before our honeymoon, but the reality was different than my daydreams.

Liz was as deeply motivated as me, it was part of the reason I felt so comfortable with her. But she could turn it off. My brain was wired a certain way, and it was my own doing. Building things and writing code was my only escape from my physical body, I quickly realized I needed some time away from our honeymoon.

Time on the beach turned to time in the pool, each of us with drinks in our hands and water as blue as the sunny skies. Liz looked stunning in the sunshine, the beautiful hues of the tropics viewed through a pair of sunglasses amplified her allure. I caught myself staring at her now and again, she was my wife now, I was more fortunate than I ever deserved. The young twitchy boy married the kind of woman I'd only dreamed of.

I was so fortunate to have her by my side, to spend time with someone who shared my drive and passion. Alongside the gratitude came the thoughts. *I need to work, I need to make something.* Back in the real world, the way I'd wired myself seemed normal, but now in the first real vacation I'd ever taken it became clear—I'm an addict—work was my drug of choice.

I saw her disappointment the first time it happened. She knew what I was, she let it slide and gave me the benefit of the doubt. Her face fell further each time. I saw a familiar look in her eyes, the concern, thinking *what is wrong with him.*

We woke up slowly. The salty air carried through our room off the ocean breeze. The sunrise's mellow oranges turned into bright yellows pouring through our seaside bungalow. I held her in my arms, our bodies completely at peace, but my mind was alive.

"Let's go read by the pool," she said, leaving the bed and throwing on a sundress.

That wouldn't suffice. She bought me a book about programming to read while we were away on vacation. It was a nice thought, but it didn't fill that same void. I didn't want to read about other people solving challenging problems, I wanted to throw my entire being at a task and see what emerged from the other side. I wanted my thoughts to fade away. Reading about code could never do that, I had to live in it.

"I'll meet you down there," I said. "Just give me a few minutes to get ready, I'll be right behind you."

She smiled at me and kissed me on the lips. The tranquil ocean in the background highlighting her blue eyes. "Just don't take too long," she said, "I get nervous being alone in a different country."

I nodded as she left the room. I sprung out of bead, pulling my laptop out of my bag. *Just a few minutes.* That was all I needed. A small problem to solve to put my mind at bay, just a small dose of code.

I opened up my screen and the synthetic glow consumed me. The sunshine felt great on my skin, but the artificial light of the screen struck a peaceful chord in me. The keyboards familiar clicks overtook the sounds of the beach, I opened up my command line, navigating through my familiar filesystem and located a small project I'd never completed. *Home is wherever my hard drive is.*

My brain came alive. The colors in the room and the warm sea air becoming fuller. Time evaporated, my physical body faded.

"Dammit Charlie!" Liz shouted. "It's been three hours!"

I stared back, knowing all too well her feelings were justified. It hurt so much more from the woman I loved. It pained me to let her down, but my mind untethered by the side of the pool was driving me mad. Every few seconds another urge to tic, every few seconds thoughts telling me I should be doing something, making something. I was broken, I needed to do the one thing I was good at, the only way I knew how to bring value into the world.

"I'm sorry," I said, pulling my eyes away and slowly closing my screen. It hurt, right in the heat of things, right when the code was coming alive. As the screen shut, I came back to reality, realizing how frustrated she was with me. I'd left her alone in a different country, at a time supposed to be dedicated to us. Tears started to well beneath her eyes. "Is this how it's always going to be with you?"

I didn't respond. I knew the answer, but I didn't have it in me to say it. Her confident posture crumpled. I stared at her, taking in the moment. It hurt watching the woman I loved so much in tears, but I deserved the hurt. She simply wanted my time and I wasn't capable of giving it to her.

"I knew you worked constantly, but I thought getting out here and being away from everything... I thought when it was just *us,* you'd be able to turn it off."

"Don't you think I want to!" I shot back, so frustrated with myself I raised my voice louder than I wanted, "I can't turn it off. I never could. This is who I am. I've tried my whole life to change that, to make myself normal, but I can't do it. This is me, Elizabeth. You don't think I want a more normal life? You don't think I want to relax like you can, enjoy sitting poolside. It isn't the way I'm wired, and it never will be."

The tears flowed from her, the guilt of knowing I caused it settling on my shoulders.

"I'm sorry," I said after the anger at myself subsided.

She wiped a tear away, "You don't need to say that."

"Yes, I do. We should be celebrating our relationship and enjoy each other's company and I keep finding things to work on. It's not fair to you, and it's not the way our relationship is going to go."

I stood up now walking over to her, taking her hand in mine, pulling her into my arms. Her warm tears began to soak through my shirt, her arms hung around me, cradling my back. I felt at home with her, she deserved so much more than me. I would have to work to be a better husband, I swore it to myself right then. I may not be able to change completely, but I had to try.

"I promise you Liz, I'm not perfect, this is who I am. I'll be there with you when it matters. I made a commitment to you, and a commitment to myself."

I felt her smile against my chest. She looked up and kissed me, the self-doubt faded. I needed to make this promise more than just words. I couldn't be so selfish anymore; this is what mattered. Here in my arms, this woman I'd watched change and grow, the future we had in front of us with its boundless potential.

I won't mess this up.

CHAPTER 25

———

The car bounced down the gravel road, my eyes pulsing every few seconds in a Tourettic outburst. Liz had fallen asleep, and I felt guilty playing music, so the silence and rhythmic vibrations of the car reminded me of a youth spent outside the big city.

I didn't mind her sleeping; it gave me time to think. Immediately after telling her about Gerhard she requested for the two of us to take a trip. Originally we planned to visit my Mom, but she was attending a conference for work. Instead we decided on a vacation in beautiful lake country, far from the hustle of the city. Underneath that lay stress, the small conversations were as relaxing and comforting as ever, but I couldn't help feeling something was off in my life.

It was the slow season, but there were still cars throughout the parking lot. After picking up keys to our cabin from the main offices we continued another quarter mile to the lodge we booked. We drove past other weekend vacationers sipping drinks on the balconies equipped with hot tubs.

"You know that's about to happen right?" said Liz as she turned around in her seat and looked at them.

"What happened to being tired and ready to relax?" I joked.

"Well, I *was* but I napped a little too much on the ride in. Someone didn't wake me up, so now you get to deal with me wide awake."

"I'm not sure I'll be able to manage."

She kissed me playfully on the cheek as the car parked itself front of the lodge. *This was going to be refreshing spending some quality time with only the two of us.*

The cabin had a rustic feel, but an electric lock system latched the door shut and lights automatically illuminated the cabin as we walked up to the front door. We both entered the cabin excited to see what our next few days held for us. I liked to think I was outdoorsy, I'd grown up in a small town, but the city has staked its claim in me. The long days spent on the computer had destroyed any hint of outdoorsman my dad once tried to instill.

Even before turning on the lights, I saw the large black space of the lake through the gigantic cabin windows. It was a clear night, the moon and stars provided enough light to see the dancing waves against the shore.

"You already look more relaxed," Liz said behind me setting down our bags.

"And what makes you think I'm relaxed? My mind could still be at work as we speak, for all you know I'm fretting about issues with the Template."

She rolled her eyes and wrapped her arms around my neck leaning her weight back. It was dark, but I could still see her pleased smile. "I can see it in your face. Set your stuff down, I'm going to figure out the hot tub."

I gave her a kiss before letting her go. The inside matched the pictures of our booking but seeing it in person brought a new sense of reality. The decor of the inside matched the outside, decorated rustic but with all the amenities of the new age. Lights embedded into the pine ceiling illuminated the entire open area, and the subtle view of the moonlit lake shone in the background.

"Bring some wine with you. I'm going to change." Liz said from the bedroom.

I put our bags down and changed into a swimming suit, splashing water into my face waking me up after the long methodic ride north. A beautiful wife in a great mood should have excited me but looking at my face in the bathroom mirror reminded me of the face I was putting on this weekend. *Something isn't right with Gerhard; he knows something he's not telling me.*

It was the only thing on my mind, I needed to make sure my worries didn't take away from our time together. I'd been so engrossed with my own selfish endeavors recently it was time to be with Liz. She was my only priority. I dried off my face and walked into the living room, past the pine picture frames and nature photos on the wall. It reminded me of the decor in my house growing up. *You've grown soft Charlie,* the voice of my dad again in my ear. I smiled slightly; I'd grown so far from my roots. This trip was something Liz and I could afford to do without a thought, nearly any weekend we pleased. I wasn't sure how

I felt being so different from the people I grew up around, Liz and I had attained a high level of success. Moments like this reminded me that my differences did have some perks.

"They already have the hot tub warmed up," Liz said, standing confidently in her swimsuit in front of me. She looked beautiful, but that word alone didn't do her justice. She was self-confident, the youth of her early twenties behind her, but her poise masked any blemishes.

I opened the fridge; it came fully stocked with food, but my eyes shot right towards the chilled wine on the bottom shelf.

"Look what I found," I said.

Liz leaned up against the island in the middle of the kitchen, playfully swaying and clearly enjoying watching me get into the spirit of the night.

"Perfect," she said.

I made my way out to the porch with a swagger of excitement in my step.

"Wait," she said right as I was about to hop in the hot tub.

"What?"

"Where is your phone?"

"It's in my bag. Why?"

She walked over to my bag and pulled it out and turned it off.

"Can you make me a promise, Charlie?" She said, her voice flirting between normal volume and a whisper.

"What's that?" I asked.

"Can we leave this off for the weekend?"

I looked at her, slightly frustrated, "I'm waiting on important news."

She stared back at me, as unrelenting as ever. As frustrating as that stubbornness was, I loved her for it.

"Till Sunday morning. No later." I said pointing my finger at it.

The software shut down with a playful little tune.

"Deal," she said, jumping on my offer immediately.

"That means you as well," I said with a coy grin on my face.

"Sure," she said rolling her eyes, "because I'm the one who has a problem taking their mind off work"

"If I have to do it you better as well."

She grabbed her phone off the counter and did the same, this time much more animated and holding her free hand on her hip.

"I hope you're happy," she said.

"I am," I said, it may have been her idea, but it would be good for us. "Only you and me this weekend, what's not to love?"

She grabbed me by the arm and dragged me out to the hot tub, still holding the bottle of wine. Liz jumped in and I followed, relaxing into the warm bubbles. The light breeze and cold air shot a life back into me in the same way seeing Liz in her bathing suit did. This was going to be a great weekend.

And it was for a time.

CHAPTER 26

———

The trails weaved around the lake, through its surrounding hills and trees. The movement of hiking melted away the stresses of Mendelium. Weathered trees craned across the winding forest paths. My lungs felt alive in the crisp fall air.

We stopped at an overlook, taking in the serene view that was so foreign to me in a typical day. Technology and code were the thing I contributed most to the world, creating a better society through software. But something felt right out here, something buried deep in my own source code. Part of my human operating system felt aligned with the fresh air and exercise.

"I told you," Liz said to me, the gentle breeze moving the tail of her loose bun.

"Told me what?"

She walked over to me, then rested her head on my shoulder. "You needed some time away. I know you love your work, but everyone needs a mental break now and again. If for nothing else, you'll have some fresh ideas when you get back into the office."

"It's been nice," I agreed. I decided it best not to tell her that for the last two miles I'd been wondering how difficult it would be to write an algorithm to mimic the lapping waves of the lake.

"When I was a girl, I always imagined moving out somewhere like this when I started a family of my own," she said.

"Speaking of..."

"Just let me finish," she said, "it's just funny how different life ends being from what you imagined. I thought I would have a couple children by now, or that we'd live out away from the city in a nice quiet life. I wonder what that girl would think of me now. Would she think me afraid?"

"Liz, I've been—"

"I'm so proud of what I've done with my time so far, I love our life together, there are parts of what we have that is so much more beautiful than that girl once dreamed of. But I still feel like something is tugging at me, something unfinished. I know how you feel, and I'll continue being patient. I understand your reprehension, but it's just been eating at me Charlie..."

"Elizabeth!"

She stopped, catching her breath, a fire still in her eyes.

"I'm ready. I'm ready to have kids."

Her face twisted into a smile, she walked back towards me, then punched me in the arm.

"Ow, what was that for?"

"Why the hell didn't you tell me sooner? You let me ramble on and on."

"I've been trying," I said, rubbing my arm.

"When did you decide?"

"I think I decided a while ago, now all the business with the Template is over. I wanted to wait until the right time to tell you." I looked around at serene lake and wispy clouds, "It seemed like the perfect moment."

"You need to stop waiting and just start telling me things Charlie. I'm not some delicate flower that everything needs to be perfect for. I just want the truth."

"Well, this is the truth, Liz. I've risked everything these last few weeks and I'm done. I've made up my mind. I'm starting to realize that I'm never going to feel ready. I'm always going to throw myself into solving the next pressing problem, but a part of me will always be with you and our family."

She looked at me for a long moment, and then wrapped her arms around me. "I'm so happy to hear you say that."

"I'm excited," I said. "I love you."

"I love you too."

I held her in my arms for a moment, looking across the lake.

"I'll finally get to wear this Template thing I keep hearing about,"she joked. "You better be damn sure that you didn't mess things up too bad."

"I promise," I laughed. "We just moved things back one version, it'll still protect us from anything going seriously wrong."

I thought about our future child and the chance they might be born with Tourette's syndrome. A part of me hoped they would share my defining feature, the tics were the backbone of so much of my life. My constant convulsive passenger.

"Good morning," said a calm voice from behind us. I jumped turning around to see an older couple walking up the trail behind us. "I hope we didn't intrude on anything; we are just enjoying this beautiful morning."

There was no doubt in my mind they were married, even from a distance they seemed to move together, their smiling faces each round and welcoming. The man reached us first, his hair almost fully transitioned from brown to grey.

"Good morning," Liz said, still beaming. "How are the two of you?"

They looked out across the lake as they reached the top of the hill. The view from above was stunning, now that the sun was higher into the sky, the waves shimmered and reflected its light. A duck took off from nearby, flapping its wings, surging out of the water. "It's like it's more beautiful each and every time we come here."

"It's our first," Liz said, smiling at me, "but I don't think it will be our last."

"Are you folks from the city?" The woman asked. I nodded.

"We used to be, but we moved further away once we retired. Brent and I miss the excitement.

"We think about that sometimes," Liz said, "whether or not we'll always live there. I seem to forget how much I love the fresh air and open spaces until we take a trip away."

"I'm Irene," the older woman said. Her hair was dark brown, with not a dash of grey, I suspected she dyed it since she looked so much like her husband in every other way.

"And I'm Brent," said the man, his belly jiggled as he walked towards me. He shook my hand and gave me a jovial smile. "I have to confess that I actually recognize you Mr. Lamarck."

"Charlie, please."

"I'm not surprised you don't recognize me, it's been years since I worked at Mendelium, but I still keep tabs on the place."

"It's been one hell of a fall."

"For you in particular," he said.

"What brings you two here?" Liz asked.

"We honeymooned out here thirty years ago," Irene said, "we make a point to come back every year. Rent a cabin and enjoy some time away."

"Wow," Liz said, "congratulations."

Her face light up as she spoke with them. Spending these days alone was nice, but Liz craved interaction with other humans more than I did. Where I preferred to be reclusive and spend time alone, she walked away invigorated from social interaction. All this time secluded was great for me, but I could tell she was craving conversation with others. I decided to take a shot in the dark.

"Would you two like to come over for dinner tonight?" I asked.

Irene and Brent looked at each other briefly, sharing a quick silent conversation in a gaze, Liz looked at me, a confused smile on her face.

"We'd love to," the two of them said in unison.

I attempted to channel young Grace Geller's budding talent, and cooked dinner for the four of us that evening. It was a miss, but they complimented me anyways as we ate and talked about how relaxing it was out here far away from our problems. Liz worked her magic, connecting with Irene and empathizing with her life. All the while I regurgitated the same small talk conversations that I'd had countless times before. Despite being a bore, Brent was kind. His rosy cheeks were nearly as red as his glass of wine. The two of them moved together as a unit, laughing at our jokes like a choreographed dance. The conversation stayed easy; I could see Liz become more comfortable the more she talked with Irene. Brent didn't have to ask me twice to have a drink with him out on the patio.

"You know," Brent began, between sips of his merlot. "I'm a bit jealous of you. Retirement has been relaxing, but I miss being part of something bigger than myself. You are so fortunate to work somewhere that makes such an impact on the world."

"I have *certainly* made an impact."

"When I was a boy, I used to dream about the future. Technology mutates and changes so rapidly, I assumed it would only continue. I figured that by the time I was this age we would be flying cars and our attachment to nature would be gone. But that's not what's happened.

"I didn't anticipate Mendelium, or the impact that genetic technologies would have on the world. When you boil it down so many of our problems can be solved by creating healthier humans. The effects of poor mental health cascade into every aspect of our world today—but what if we can simply eliminate them? I never would have seen this solution. But now every government in the world is throwing money at

Mendelium, they are all hoping to stop their problems at their root level."

I nodded along with him, trying to mask my tics.

"Instead of melding human with machine, we use machines to grow better humans. Nature and technology intertwined to solve our problems. You are creating a world where elders can live longer and better pass along their expertise to those with their youth. Removing Alzheimer's and dementia is comparable to rediscovering the Library of Alexandria. Future generations can continue to grow using the knowledge passed down to them. You are quite literally building a better human race."

I ticced again as I listened to him wax poetic about the company I'd just attempted to hamstring.

"You always so jumpy?" he asked leaning against the railing looking over the lake. Even after hiking around the entire body of water, it still looked beautiful.

"Tourette's syndrome," I said, ready for the conversation I'd been forced to have so many times before.

"But I haven't heard you shout or swear or anything?" He asked.

"The swearing thing is called coprolalia. Only a few people with Tourette's syndrome swear like that. Most of us just blink a lot or have other weird twitches."

"Oh," Brent said, taking another drink. *No one ever did know how to react to that.*

"They get worse sometimes, if I'm stressed out or not sleeping well."

"So? Which is it? You are off on a beautiful weekend with your wife, I can't imagine you aren't sleeping well."

"Stress," I said, after brief pause.

"I hope Irene and I aren't the cause of that," he said, his eyes were soft and he looked genuinely concerned. I was wrong about him at first glance. Though he seemed overly masculine, he was genuinely interested in Liz and I. He followed each question with curious eyes and a kindhearted smile.

"You and Irene are great," I said, taking a swig of my drink. "I've been struggling to take my mind off of work."

"Having a coworker murdered could do that to a person," he said looking out onto the lake. The waves began to crash harder against the beach below as the cool evening air rolled in.

"It's not just that, things are changing. The last meeting, I had with Gerhard didn't go well, I'm not sure what I'm coming back to."

"I'm sure it'll be something you can endure," he said. "If Gerhard can continue on after Carmen's death, then nothing will stop that man from getting what he wants."

"Were you around back then when she... you know..."

"I was," Brent said, drinking the last of his wine. "People think Gerhard looks fractured physically, but it's nothing compared to what happened to him when he found her. He's barely even the same man today."

"That's hard to believe," I said. "He still operates at a level I can barely comprehend."

"He's doing incredible things for the world, but he's not the well-meaning savior he's cracked up to be. He's got his secrets like anyone else."

I listened intently, the warm buzz of alcohol filling my body.

"I met Carmen once in the early days of Mendelium. She had one of the kindest souls—this world simply isn't fair."

"I can't imagine how difficult that would have been." I said, "I've always felt terrible for Gerhard and Grace, to go through something like that."

"I don't think it was quite so simple," Brent said, "word travels throughout a company, some people believe her death was his fault."

"But she killed herself," I said in rebuttal.

"Yes, but none of us know the details about what happened inside their relationship. Gerhard came out looking great to everyone in the press. All the employees at Mendelium acted so sympathetic for their fearless leader without knowing about what happened between the two of them.

"He was controlling. Changing your own child's genetics and hiding it from your wife? There is no way I could ever forgive that."

"Well, he created Mendelium, of course he's going to use his own technologies when Grace was born."

"There was rumors he did other things too, things he kept even from Carmen. Can you even imagine your whole world being manipulated right under your nose? The audacity to experiment with your own child and keep it hidden from your wife? I meet with a lot of people in my line of work, never have I met someone who would do that."

"What exactly did he do to her?"

"I don't know. Some people think that he enhanced certain features of hers, or that he gave her experimental traits they wouldn't allow anyone else to have."

My perceptions of the man shift beneath me, like standing at the top of a skyscraper during a gust of wind. My whole life felt slightly less stable. I tried to hide it from my face, but it was there for him to see.

"But that's the way life is," he said. "No one is perfect, Gerhard is a tortured man, but at least he's using his life to build a better humanity. You can't help but feel sorry for him, his pain has been a boon to the rest of us."

"But enough with the gossip," Brent said. "What is next on the horizon for you and Elizabeth? You've been married for a while now. Are kids next? Irene and I..."

I nodded along, but his words fell into the background. My gears spinning, thinking back to earlier conversations Gerhard. Grasping for something.

Was that what I'd seen in his eyes when Gerhard looked at Grace? Something was off. Why would he ever feel the need to hide something? It was his life's work, of course he would give his daughter every advantage in life. Did he regret what he had done? He was skeptical about the future of the Template, and I thought that was the whole story. But the Template was connected to his daughter in a way I hadn't realized before. I needed to speak with him. Something in Brent's story didn't add up.

"Charlie?" he asked, "are you alright?"

"I'm sorry, my stomach is bothering me, I'll be right back."

I went to our bedroom; the large space began to feel like a home away from home even though we still had our suitcase out on the table and clothes scattered across the floor. *What if part of the reason he wanted*

*me away was so he could operate without me in prox-
imity?* The sliver of trust I had was now gone, nothing
had changed, yet the entire situation felt different. I'd
placed my entire trust in Gerhard, I'd just accepted
his word as truth. Had I been wrong?

He just wanted me to get my mind right, but a quick
check wouldn't do any harm. I pressed the power button and the phone lit up. Immediately vibrations and
noises poured out. Twenty three missed calls, and
countless new messages.

Shit.

"Liz," I shouted.

"What?" she asked, a smile still on her face as she
came into the bedroom.

"We have to go. Now."

Her smile fell; her expression moved past confusion directly to anger when she saw the phone in
my hand.

I began frantically packing everything into our
suitcase. I closed my eyes, the texts felt like a burst
of sobriety. We had to go.

"What in the *hell.*" Liz said, her face saying the
words before she did.

"Something's happened. I'll tell you on the way
there, we need to leave."

"Brent and Irene are sitting on our porch right now
and we've been having a lovely night, they were telling
me about their sons—"

"Elizabeth, we have to go. Tell them what you need
to and help me finish packing, I will be right back."

I rushed out of the room and through the front
door, right past Brent and Irene, both flashed me

big smiles as I ignored them and bolted out into the night. The crisp air and laughter from the cabins now completely lost to me. It was minutes before I even realized I was running. Racing past the cabins, some with their lights still on and some dark. I reached the member's services center and started banging on the door.

"Hey, you don't need to do that," said the desk attendant that checked us in yesterday, his dirty blond hair covering his left eye. He frowned and opened the door, "What's wrong?"

"We have to check out, tonight."

"Sir, are you sure it can't wait? Come tomorrow morning there will be— "

"I need to get back to the city. Now. I don't care if we can't get a refund," I said.

"I suppose it's not a problem, I can stay open for a few more minutes, just drop off your keys on your way out."

"I have to head back and finish packing things up."

He nodded still looking unsure about the whole situation.

I ran down the wooded trail past the cabins, deep breaths of cold air cut through my lungs. It took a few minutes to get the last of our stuff thrown in the car, Liz was ready to go by the time I got back, Brent and Irene long gone. She hopped in beside me still sporting a look of concern. The self-driving car cruised through the winding paths of the resort and out onto the highway.

"Charlie," Liz stated, her tone so cold compared the rest of the day. "You need to tell me what is going on."

"James is in jail."

"Wait, what for?" Liz said, eyes large and white even in the darkness.

"The murder of Dave Lattimore."

CHAPTER 27

———

SIX MONTHS EARLIER

James and I sat through the celebration. Another successful round of Template production, another cross section of the human genome removed.

"You'd think being one of the fastest-growing companies in the world we'd be able to pay for this thing ourselves," James said. The two of us strolled around the edges of the party, looking across the sprawling green hills of the country club, peppered with white sand bunkers and carefully manicured trees.

"Whenever I start to think I understand rich people, something happens that makes me feel like I have no idea," I said.

"Why is that?" he asked.

"With Mendelium rolling in cash you would think we would be footing the bill, but it seems like the richer you are the more other rich people want to give things away to you."

James chuckled as people came in and out of the party. Women in heels and shining necklaces, men with watches more valuable than most cars. Three large tents wrapped around the side of the country club. Their normal services closed for the party.

"Is this really what the American Cancer Foundation's donors wanted their money spent towards? A bunch of rich people posturing for news stories?"

"Life isn't only about getting things done Charlie, business, and pretty much everything in life revolves around who you know. They might be wealthy, but some of these people have done a lot of good for the world. Rich people are just people. Some good, some bad, their money just serves as an amplifier. If someone is an ass and they get rich they'll just start posturing and using their money to fill whatever voids are missing from their lives. Good rich people exist though, a few of them are even walking around this party."

Gerhard sat underneath one of the closer tents, his wheelchair planted in the center with a line of people coming up to him for handshakes and greetings. Each thrilled to introduce themselves to the man who claimed to have eliminated prostate and breast cancer from the gene pool.

"I'm sorry I like to get things done with my time on this planet rather than flash a smile and wear a face I think others will like."

"Some of the most important moments in history have been conversations," James said, "Ideas transferring from one person to another take place in spaces like this one. It may not be your world, but there's no denying important discussions have their place."

He gestured out towards the golf course, the setting sun casting long shadows on the tents in front of us. We looked across it, I was grateful to have him here with me, someone to talk to at these things. Without him I would feel alienated among this affluent crowd.

"How does it seem to just happen for some people?" I asked. "How do the words come so easily for you?"

"Some are blessed I suppose, but there are similarities to computer programming you know. At its core, conversation is a skill, something you can practice and refine. You are looking at some of the most elite people in their domains, they may not perform on a court or a field, but they are highly practiced at their sport of choice."

I nodded, looking through the crowds of people making small talk and posturing towards one another. All the while waiting staff in white weaved throughout the crowds.

"Just like with code there is infrastructure to set up first. You can't simply walk in and be charming—you need connections—relationships built on years of rapport. You have invested in your skill Charlie, your countless hours of programming, and created a business for the world. My investments are different, they walk around and speak to one another. But they still compound over time. People think guys like you and I would be so different, but at the core we are all doing the same thing. Honing our craft one day at a time.

"When you worked at GeniSense you created a niche. You focused all your efforts on one specific market. Well, I've done the same. I'm the guy that can get you things, that reputation is something I've cultivated, it's the reason I'm so well connected. My investments are starting to pay off."

He was right. Did he look at me in the same way I did him? Jealous of the path not taken. I'd been single-mindedly pursuing the things in front of me, never once looking up to see others were following paths of their own. I loved my work, but I envied James's people skills with every fiber in my body. In the moment I loved what I did, I loved the way the tics melted away as the code formed together in my mind. What if I had taken a different path? Could I ever truly change the world like one of these people with their smiles and calculated laughs?

James threw back the last of his drink.

"Time to tend to the investments?" I asked.

He smiled back at me, straightening up his posture with his normal swagger and confidence, "Time to work."

CHAPTER 28

The guard opened the door to the visitation room. James' normally well-tailored suit replaced with a baggy grey prison uniform. His face locked in a frown, when he saw us the corner of his mouth slowly formed into a welcoming grin, but the twinkle in his eye was dim.

The science labs at Mendelium Tower were nothing like their Hollywood counterparts, I shouldn't have expected the prison to look like the ones in the movies either. It wasn't the dark ominous space I was anticipating. The walls were painted a light green. The floors so clean they shined as much as the bald head of an inmate talking to his daughter across the room.

"It's good to see you both," he said. His once-booming voice fell flat in the sterile room.

What was I supposed to say? I felt guilty, I wasn't there for him when he called.

Liz walked up and hugged him, and the bailiff off to the side looked on disapprovingly. "No contact." He grumbled after she released him.

"Thank you for coming," he said, "I—I need to talk with somebody, somebody who will actually listen to what I have to say."

"We are here for you," I said, trying to convey my worry in a glance.

"I know you are. How was your vacation? Did you two enjoy your time away?"

"James!" Liz exclaimed, "That's not important right now, what happened? Tell us everything."

"I need to come clean about some things," he said looking down at his hands. Even his fingers didn't look like his own, they were grimy with dirt shoved up underneath his normally neat fingernails. "I tried calling you like ten times."

"Twelve," I corrected, feeling a deep pang of guilt.

"I think I killed Dave," he said.

"How can you not know?" Liz asked.

"I believe I was set up."

The situation was frustrating, but it didn't override the years of trust and friendship we shared. I'd been on high alert since arriving here, searching his face for any sign he might be hiding something from me. Nothing. The same James I had always known sat across from me, perhaps more exhausted and flustered than I'd ever known him to be. The man who tried his hardest to reach me right before being arrested. He deserved my time, he deserved an open mind.

"What makes you think that?" I asked.

He closed his eyes and began to speak, the words seemed like they hurt as they came out. "I want you to understand, in order for me to do that you have to know about my relationship with Dave. I hate being called a drug dealer, you know that isn't how any of this started. I pride myself in helping people operate at their highest level. But Dave wanted harder things. Things I wasn't comfortable with. I told him no—I must have told him no over a hundred times. But his persistence eventually turned into threats."

"He threatened you?" Liz questioned.

"He did, which makes this all the harder, because it gives me a motive. He threatened to expose me. He got video of me selling to coworkers."

"That sounds like Dave," I said. "How did he set you up?"

"One thing at a time," he said, his tone still seemed hollow. The normal smile and laugh absent from his face. "Dave approached me for a specific reason. Quality. He'd been burned in the past. He knew I had good connections, and that I tested meticulously."

I nodded along, I was watching Liz, curious if she was any less angry with me now for checking my phone and ripping us away from our vacation.

"It was a habit I got into early on, I had an experiment with performance enhancers go wrong in college. Went to the hospital thinking I was having a heart attack, turns out the central nervous system stimulant I took was laced with something stronger. I developed much better sources after that. Carefully testing all of the products I purchased and making connections with people who sold the highest quality stuff."

"Yet you continued to do them?" Liz questioned with narrowed eyes.

"I did, and I stand by that decision. What I didn't continue to do however was use them haphazardly.

I've tried to be discreet about my dealings, but Dave uncovered everything. If Bill and Mike hadn't searched so thoroughly through Dave's computer and began pulling at strings they never would have found out."

"You gave Dave some bad drugs I'm guessing?"

"I made the purchase the day beforehand. I had to. Dave requested an inordinate amount, threatening me if I didn't follow through. So, I hit up my dealer and set up an appointment."

"The same one you normally do?"

"The very same."

"And?" Liz asked.

"It went as expected, and I tested the product diligently. Everything went according to plan. I have...," he trailed off, eyeing the corrections officer standing in the corner, "I *had* a safe system and pressure sensors surrounding it. I would know if someone messed with it."

"Was anything different?"

"No. I'm careful about where I keep my product. If something was tampered with it's my business to know. I have security cameras surrounding my home, and logs of everything happening around my safe room."

"The cameras," Liz said, "did you see anything on them?"

"Nothing," James hung his head again. "I don't see how this could have happened. He didn't die because of anything I gave him."

He played with his thumbs again, looking down and talking, "I know how this must seem Charlie, all I'm asking for is a little help, I have no one else."

"You're certain that's what killed him?" Liz chimed in.

"The police are."

"And they have a video of you talking about dealing to him?" Liz said leaning into the conversation.

"Sure do."

"Shit."

"Shit," he said back to me. This time I saw the fear his smile was trying to hide.

"Who do you think it was?" Liz asked, I could see her wheels spinning.

"I have theories, but I don't see any motivation. I was hoping you might have some ideas. There isn't a chance Dave's wife could have orchestrated something like that, even if she did find out about his past. It has to be someone at Mendelium, someone with something to gain from his death."

"I don't know," I responded, but I knew it wasn't true. I had no proof, no motive, nothing foundational. But I felt something in my gut I couldn't shake. *I needed to speak with Gerhard.*

"I agree with you. There has to be someone at Mendelium with motive," Liz said decisively.

"Is there anyone else involved with Dave?" I asked.

"The cops have been investigating this for weeks and I'm the only person they found anything against."

"Hmm" I said, letting my mind run, "I could see financial incentives for someone on the board to have him killed."

"Could you talk to Gerhard?" James asked, "I know how close the two of you have become, meeting all the time in the office after hours and stuff."

"We… our relationship isn't what it used to be," I said. *Is Gerhard involved somehow?* Our plan wouldn't have happened if he didn't have my help, it was me that gave the speech, it was me that did all of the legwork. There was too much going on right now. Behind a computer, my mind seemed to work perfectly, but here, in a situation with people I loved, I felt like I couldn't think. The tics flooded over me, in some moments, they seemed to shake my whole body, the neck twitch and the eye twitch combining into a symphony of spasms.

"Could you do it anyways? You're all I've got now C," James pushed again.

"Something is about to happen at Mendelium." I said. "Something big. There are other things in play right now that must take priority."

"I don't have anyone else," he said growing frustrated.

"Look James, I know where you are coming from—"

"The hell you do," James yelled, "You know? You can't know. I would have expected you to be taking my side on this."

The guard standing calm at the door fighting his drooping eyelids was now on James, securing him and pulling him back away from the table.

"I'm fine, I'm fine," James shouted.

"You're done," said the guard, gesturing for James to leave the room.

"Charlie, this is all I've got. I need you. Please. Someone is trying to frame me, I'm sure of it."

The guard forced James out of the room. Liz and I sat there in silence, with no idea where to go from here.

CHAPTER 29

I walked down the sidewalk through the old parts of the city. Near the old GeniSense offices—through a mountain of regret from my past life. The sun was soft in the evening sky as I approached Liz's building. I passed into the brick entryway engulfed by flowering white vines. The lower floors of the building were empty as I climbed the stairs to the top.

Her floor was quiet too. It looked like all her employees left the office for the day; the desks vacant except for the papers and computers strewn atop them. The refurbished building's red bricks lining the entire length of the office. The light of the afternoon and noises from the city below seeped through the windows.

I saw her before she did me. Her office was perched over the rest of the floor, with glass walls surrounding her to match with the open concept of the rest of the office. I loved seeing her in this environment, so different from the Liz I spend time with at home. She sat at the throne of the company she had built on her own, working long and hard after the rest of her employees went home for the weekend.

She typed on the keyboard, her focus clearly immersed on the task at hand. I watched her smile light up as she noticed me. *That feeling would never get old.*

"You did come," she said, as she looked away from her screen.

"I said I would, I don't have much else to do right now."

"I'm jealous," she said, "I was hoping to get away from my desk for lunch, but I've already missed that by a few hours."

"Doesn't mean you can't get away for dinner with your loving husband. We can celebrate a little bit, maybe even grab a couple of drinks. I for one could certainly use one."

"What exactly are we celebrating?" she asked. "Did you speak to Gerhard? Is there any news about James?"

"Still no," I said, pushing down that familiar gut feeling that I wouldn't be able to do anything to help James, "but there still is something to celebrate."

She continued to look on at me curious, now leaning back in her chair, her dark red top emphasizing the red of her lip stick.

"We can celebrate you and me. We can celebrate starting a family together."

Her confused face twisted into a smile. "So, it's really happening then? It wasn't just vacation talk?"

"Of course not," I said walking around her desk and reaching out my hand. She grabbed it and I pulled her up to her feet, placing both of my hands on her sides. I fell into her gaze, feeling like a stronger version of myself in their focus.

"I don't know why I second guessed you," she began, "with everything else happening with James and Gerhard I though the stress might make you doubt the timing again."

"There is no more doubt," I said, staring into her soft blue eyes. "I'm done putting what we have at risk, I'm ready to move onto the next phase of our life."

She grabbed my hands and smiled up at me. A lock of her honey blonde hair falling in between her face and mine, we stood there in the quiet office. I saw our entire future and past in her gaze, the woman that was now the at the center point of everything important in my life. Right now the sweetness of reality was better than delving into code.

I ran my fingers through her hair as she placed her hands on my chest. Her touch reminding me of just how cold and lonely my life had been before she entered it. I remembered that phase of my world, the Charlie that walked into the coffee shop all those years ago. The same warmth that ran though me then ran through me again now.

She kissed me. The sounds of the world outside her office stopped. The only thing that I cared about was wrapped up in my arms. I tasted the sweetness of her lips, the familiar sound of her breath so close to mine.

She lingered for a second and then pulled away.

"So where are we going out for dinner?" She asked, holding her arms around me, and looking up at me.

I didn't respond.

The only thing I could think about was the way her hands rested around me. I kissed her again, letting myself get swept away in the moment. Our life was changing, and right now we were at the center of it. She hesitated briefly, and then kissed me back. I felt the corners of her mouth turned up into a smile as I pulled her into me. Letting all reason and logic in my life fall away.

My heart pulsed we locked together. Starting a family brought a new level of nervousness—and with it an intoxicating thrill.

She bit at my lip and squeezed her legs up and around me. The two of us fell onto her desk, the warmth of her skin emanating through our clothes.

I didn't look up or around to see if anyone was there. I didn't care. The only person that mattered to me right now was her, pressed between me and the thick wooden desk. She ran her hands through my hair as the two of us embraced, locked together in each other's arms.

Slowly, the orange rays of the sun sank across the city.

CHAPTER 30

EIGHTEEN YEARS EARLIER

"Stop fiddling with your tie, honey."

"I can't mom, it's choking me." I pulled at it, the fabric rough against my skin. "Why do I even have to wear this thing? Dad hated ties."

"He loved the way you looked when you dressed up. You won't have to wear it much longer."

The bright greens of early spring flashed past the car windows as I stared into the distance. I didn't want to look at Mom anymore, the red marks around her eyes were beginning to feel permanent. I couldn't glance at her without remembering how much our life changed.

We parked the car in front of the funeral home, the large brick building located on the outskirts of the city. She smiled at me as we got out, a thin veneer over the heartache that lived beneath. I smiled back, wondering if she could see how fractured I was too.

We approached the doors, lined with freshly manicured bushes. They tried so hard to make the place look beautiful. But it was only temporary, by the end of the summer all their leaves would wither away. Just a poor attempt to make us forget our sorrows.

I followed Mom to the door but hesitated at the entrance. People kept telling me that a funeral was for closure, but the last thing in the world I wanted was to forget about him. I wanted to hang on to every part of his memory. I ticced. Flexing my jaw and snapping my neck to the side.

I forced myself through the entryway and into the interior of the brick building. It felt claustrophobic. The small area was packed with friends and family and the ceilings barely cleared some of my taller relatives' heads.

A group of my cousins congregated near the door. They exchanged glances when they saw Mom and I enter. One of my distant older cousins approached first. She wore a long black dress, tears pulled the mascara down her face, drawing even more attention to her over-the-top fake eyelashes. It had been years since we'd last spoke and I couldn't remember her name.

"Oh Charlie," she said as she ran up to me and embraced me in a hug. "You poor thing."

I resisted the initial urge to pull back, I didn't want to be touched, but she looked even more emotionally distraught than me. Everyone looked on as she wept on my shoulder.

"I can't believe it, I feel like I was just talking with your dad weeks ago. I'll never hear one of Uncle Calvin's jokes again. I'm lost Charlie, but we can get through this together."

"Sure," I said, hoping she would take the cue to leave me alone.

"I've been completely beside myself since I found out. I don't know how I'm going to move on."

"Well I'm sure we'll find a way to manage," I said with a tight lipped smile. I walked past her, on through the rows of family and friends. I felt the familiar presence of watchful eyes. These people didn't just look at me because of my spasming jaw, they were curious. Some gave me warm glances as I walked past, other eyes darted away when they saw Mom and I had finally arrived.

The warmth of the room felt so fake, the candles and flowers just a facade. The funeral director moved around the room, ushering people to their seats, for them it was just another day on the job.

His casket sat open across the room. I moved towards it cautiously. He looked *wrong*. It was still my father, but all of the details were off. They trimmed his mustache a little too thin and parted his hair the wrong way. There was makeup caked on his cheeks trying to cover up his gaunt face.

He should have been laughing, he should have been breathing. This empty thing wasn't my father anymore. I flexed my jaw as my neck spasmed, letting the tears pour down. Emotions were just a tic, another bodily urge outside of my conscious control. I didn't care if the others saw the tears any more than I cared if they saw my tics, this was who I was. This is who my dad wanted me to be. I let the emotions come and I wept beside him.

I reached into my pocket and pulled out one of the fortune cookies we used to open and read to each other, then carefully tucked it into his pocket. His body was stiff and cold. "We should have read so many more of these together Dad. I thought we had more time."

"Calvin Lamarck has passed away." My uncle said from the stage, "A great man who brought joy to everyone he interacted with."

He wore a mustache just like my father's. It felt unfair to see him still alive. Why did Dad lose the genetic lottery and he win? They had the same parents. It wasn't right that this world took my father while an older version of him still lived.

Mom followed. I felt completely in sync with her, the two of us inseparable since he passed, like two computer screens mirroring one another. Seeing her break down in front of the crowd reminded me of how permanently this would affect our family. Were we even a family anymore? From now on it would just be the two of us.

She finished and it was my turn. I thought back to my last presentation in front of the class, there were no nerves, today I was steady. It didn't matter what any of them thought. I didn't care. I *couldn't* care.

"My dad is dead," I said as I looked across the crowd of mismatched family. "Those words hurt to say, because more than anything I don't want them to be real. I keep thinking that if I just let myself fall asleep, I might wake up in a world where he and I can spend another day together.

"I'll always remember the Saturday mornings watching cartoons and eating pancakes. I'll remember going to the movies and sneaking in as much candy as we could fit in both of our pockets. I have countless memories of a life cut far too short. I'll always remember him, but I'm scared I'm going to forget to see the world like he did. Dad forced me to find the silver lining, even his final words were a reminder that I needed to see the good side of life and embrace who I was.

"He may have died, but we can still give his life meaning. There is nothing we can do to bring him back, the only option we have is to let a piece of him live on in each of us. We must carry his memory with us through the world.

"I've always hated the tics, I hate the way my brain fights a constant battle against my body. But for my entire life he challenged me to view them as a positive.

"You're not with us anymore, Dad, but I swear to you, and in front of each and every person here today—I'm going to try. He may have left this world, but he's only truly gone if we let his impact on each of us fall away. I refuse to do that. I will fight against my own self-doubt just like I fight against the constant intrusive tics every moment of my life."

Right on cue another Tourettic outburst echoed through me, my jaw flexed and snapped to the side. I looked to his casket, towards the shell of the man I loved.

"I love you so much, Dad. And for the rest of my life, I promise to carry you with me."

CHAPTER 31

———

The atmosphere was so much different than it was at my own father's funeral. The sky a lighter blue, the frigid breeze carried thousands of fall leaves between the gravestones. Hundreds gathered in the tree laden cemetery. There was a tension in the air, and something artificial behind it. Among the somber faces were smiles, so many people in the crowd were here to keep up appearances. It felt more like a meeting up in Mendelium's offices than it did a funeral.

Salesmen shook hands and smiled, their phony husbands and wives posed at their sides. *I wish Liz was here.* She always helped me navigate awkward conversations, but her firm was hosting their biggest wedding of the year today. Without James around the crowds of Mendelium felt more isolating than ever. Of course people like Li or Hayes never seemed to get invites to events like this one. I was alone.

Most of Mendelium moved across the damp grass, crowded around the grave. The funeral had been delayed for months because of the criminal investigation, but today Dave's family would finally get closure. I was required to attend, to show my face and play my role as board member, but I had a secondary motive. *James didn't kill Dave.* I kept seeing his face in my mind across from the prison room table, the strain of being misunderstood reflecting in his eyes. All he wanted was for me to believe him, I owed him that. But it led to a distressing realization.

The killer was free.

They were likely nearby, wandering through the wilted flowers and gravestones of the long forgotten. It couldn't have been random, someone at Mendelium must have been involved. Maybe if I approached them in person and saw the movements of their eyes, perhaps I could glimpse into their source code and understand their intentions.

The hearse drove past the crowd. I ticced. The small spasm was nothing compared to the convulsive jaw clenching tics at my father's funeral. Like a wave cresting over the beach the feeling dissipated. That was a lifetime ago, a different person. The man I'd become rooted in the wishes of my father. *You must learn to love the tics Charlie; they are part of who you are.* No longer did I doubt those words. No longer where they an idea. They crystalized into a part of my being, forming the spine of Charlie Lamarck. They'd shifted from mantra into something more. It was a fundamental truth of my world. There wasn't anything *wrong* with me.

I still carried that part of him with me today. No longer the twitchy little boy afraid to stand in front of his class, but a confident man whose advantages in life were afforded by his affliction. The tics made me. There was no way I could let society remove that gift from the world. They could only look at my physical body, spasming against my control, but they didn't see the fire they created inside my mind, my syndrome was a blessing. My actions ensured future generations might learn to feel the same way.

Gerhard and Anthony cross the field of people dressed in black. His stoic face fit right in with the dim mood of the funeral, Anthony lagged, wearing an expensive suit, flashing his overly white smile. I glared in their direction, but Gerhard didn't meet my eyes, it still felt like he was avoiding me. I had to find a way to speak with him. Perhaps before the service started, I could ask him what he thought about James' arrest.

I moved through the crowd, my eyes blinking rapidly every few seconds. Past the brown-nosing managers and posturing underlings. My footfalls quiet in the dewy morning grass.

James is innocent. Should I say it outright? I'd spent so much of these last few months living selfishly. Changing the world in the way I wanted it to change. That part of my life would end. Liz and I would start a family. I had to stop focusing on what I wanted and start worrying about something bigger than myself. It didn't matter if it made me sound foolish, James had always been a friend to me, I owed him every ounce of effort I could afford. I had to confront Gerhard. It didn't matter if it was a funeral, it didn't matter if he didn't want to talk. For the sake of my friend, I would put my own concerns aside and do what was required of me.

"How dare you come here," said a shrill voice behind me. I spun around attempting to place a face to the voice, "How do you have the gall to show up?" she said again. It was Cynthia, Dave's wife. Her mascara was pulled down her face by fresh tears, it reminded me of my cousin all those years ago. Two young boys stood behind her, each bearing a slight resemblance to Dave.

I just stared back for a moment, unsure what to say, hoping that words would form in my mouth. They didn't.

"I know you were friends with him," she said with venom in her voice. "I saw you two together before, when you got awarded his position. His death has been fruitful for you, hasn't it?"

"I swear..." I began, "it's not like that, I never wanted your husband's job."

"Like hell you didn't. One of the most prestigious positions at Mendelium, I'm sure you tried your hardest to turn it down."

Just breathe Charlie. She's been through hell and is looking for someone to blame it on, you can bare it for a moment, just move on and let her get back to grieving.

"No, I am grateful, the position is something I should be proud of. Your husband worked very hard to earn the title of Board Member."

"So, you're *grateful* my husband is dead?"

I tried conveying sympathy through my gaze, but my eyes spasmed in a Tourettic outburst. "No, no, that's not what I mean."

"He was your *friend*, the one who got my husband addicted to illegal drugs, the one responsible for his overdose!"

"I don't believe James was responsible for that."

Immediately I could tell it was the wrong thing to say. Her anger swelled up inside her as she shot me a piercing glare, the small talk of the funeral quieted as more of the guests focused on the man Dave's wife was yelling at.

"You don't say his name here again. Do you understand? He was arrested," she shot. More people were coming to her aid now and standing behind her, a crowd of people dressed in black surrounding us in the graveyard. "Are you telling me that you disagree with the police? That man murdered my husband, I will *not* have you defending him at my husband's funeral."

Who was I to disagree? It was her husband, her family, the entire company that Dave was so tightly intertwined with. My eyes spasmed again with the stress of the crowd around me bearing in. I thought of James, completely alone in a prison cell, now experiencing the feeling of aloneness so familiar to me. I looked around, not seeing a single face that I truly cared about. I wouldn't let his crowd of people control what I said, what mattered was my friend and respecting his honor.

"Yes," I said back, ensuring my voice was confident and strong enough for the entire congregation to hear. "James is innocent, he may have done something morally questionable, but he would never have hurt your husband intentionally."

I stared back at her, watching the rage bubble up inside her irises. I waited for a response as she stepped closer. Instead, she swung at me, her open palm snapping across my jaw. The slap echoed over the silent crowd. All my senses switched off and anger swept over me.

"Get. The. Hell. Out." She barked. Muscular hands grabbed me from behind, forcing me through the crowd. Dragged in front of everyone. I didn't feel humiliated, but liberated. I did what was right, I spoke my mind and defended the honor of my friend, even if its cost was my own.

CHAPTER 32

———

"Well don't you look chipper," Liz said as I entered the kitchen, the smell of breakfast wafted through the house. She sported jeans and a t-shirt with her hair in a loose bun. I looked out the window. The morning sun reflected off the snow and lighting up the entire kitchen, the sounds of the television echoing through the house.

"My beautiful wife is making breakfast for me. What's not to love?"

I hoped the kind words would help to elevate my mood. They didn't. My best friend had been in prison for months now, and I couldn't shake a feeling of restlessness surrounding his upcoming trial.

Bacon and eggs sizzled on the stove while Liz made pancakes on the griddle. She moved swiftly through the kitchen with the news flickering in the background.

"How do you think you are going to do it?" She asked, floating between the stove and the pan with sizzling bacon. Spatula in one hand, a half-full coffee mug in the other.

"I plan to eat a few strips of bacon first, then grab a pancake or two afterwards. It depends on what kind you make though."

The corner of her mouth curled up into a smile, "I *meant* how are you going to confront Gerhard?"

"Ah," I said, taking a seat at the counter, "well that is going to be slightly more complicated. First and foremost, I'm going to spend a slow Saturday morning with my wife."

She smiled back at me. Something was different between the two of us, the stresses of these last few months had changed us. I watched her move through the kitchen, so grateful she'd been patient with me through all of this.

Gerhard was avoiding me. He'd been out of the country for weeks at a time and even when he was in the building Anthony wouldn't take my messages. I couldn't wait any longer, James' trial date was getting closer each week. But I had an idea. He would be at home this weekend, away from the prying eyes of Mendelium. A perfect opportunity to speak one on one.

"You better make sure to say hi to Grace for me," Liz said. "I like Gerhard and all, but I'm going to be heartbroken if I don't get to see her again just because of some argument between you and her father."

"I still have no idea what happened," I said. "It came out of nowhere, he decided to cut ties with me."

"You say that, but I know you Charlie. You probably said something harsh and rubbed him the wrong way. Please promise me you'll be quick to apologize, okay?"

"I promise," I said. Maybe she was right. What if it was something I said that upset him, my intuition told me that wasn't the case.

"Well if you do see Grace, tell her—"

"What?" I asked after she'd stopped mid-sentence and her head snapped towards the television.

"Did you hear that?"

"Hear what?"

"Something about Mendelium Tower..." she trailed off, looking around for the remote and turned the volume up so we could listen.

"—the Template might be defective. Here is Claudia Nelson with more on this worrying discovery."

"Thank you, Steven, two families have now come forward with deep concern about the effectiveness of Mendelium's crowning product, The Template. Trista and Matthew Henning recently received shocking news during their first trimester screening."

The cameras cut away to an earlier interview, what must have been Trista Henning in tears still in her hospital gown.

"That's exactly what a stressed mother-to-be needs," Liz interjected, "a bright light and camera in her face."

"We hadn't even considered the possibility of something going wrong," Trista said through heavy tears. "This will be our third child, and of course we used the Template with the first two. It wasn't a question this time around."

The camera cut back to Claudia Nelson, prepped and ready to give another rehearsed line of breaking news.

"Here at the Cumberland Hospital, the Henning family is concerned about their future. Trista's screening revealed the first case of Down syndrome since the Template's creation. It raised the question, has this been happening elsewhere? Could more family's futures be in jeopardy?"

The camera cut away again, this time to a hollow faced man in a dark shirt and tie that exaggerated his pale complexion. He sat in an armchair in an office.

"We've begun encouraging families to contact us if they notice anything strange with their pregnancies. Already we've had people come forward with concerns. At this time we are continuing to collect as much data as possible on the situation."

Liz looked at me with wide eyes. The camera panned out on Claudia Nelson this time and I recognized where she was. The concrete pathway seemed so familiar up close, now I realized it was a few hundred feet from where I exited the subway on my morning commute.

"No comment has been made from anyone at Mendelium. Our team informs us that a press conference will be held shortly, with Gerhard Geller himself slated to make a statement."

This shouldn't have happened. It should be subtle, over time, unrecognizable to anyone who wasn't paying close attention. Tourette's syndrome should have been the only condition getting through, everything else should still be functioning as expected.

"Tell me this wasn't you, Charlie. Does this have something to do with what you and Gerhard did?"

"I'm not sure. It couldn't…. it shouldn't be unless something went wrong."

"Could you have miscalculated?" she asked her bright face now completely flushed with fear.

I shook my head and stood up abruptly, "I don't think so."

I left the comforting smells of the kitchen and ran up the wooden stairs into the office. It took me a moment to find the box, I threw it open and pulled out some of the Templates I had been experimenting with. Everything looked right. There was nothing that could have failed so terribly. I flew back down the stairs, the knob of the railing wobbled as I used it to swing around the corner into the living room. *I need to talk to Gerhard.* Before his interview, before he spoke with anyone else.

"I don't know Liz, but if something did go wrong this is on me, it's going to be my fault."

"Hey," she said sternly, looking as in control as ever despite her relaxed outfit, "Focus. You need to take a moment and think clearly."

"That's a bit hard right now," I said as the weight of my actions began to settle in, my eyes watered, the sockets around them feeling heavy on my face. I couldn't sit down, instead I paced back and forth across the room.

"What are you going to do?" she asked me cautiously as I moved from one side of the room to the other.

"I need to talk to Gerhard. I have to get his opinion on all of this, he and I are both in a rough position. I love you, but I don't think you can say anything to comfort me right now. Maybe he knows something I don't, maybe I don't need to worry."

"I hope that's true," she said.

I patted on my chest and pants pockets, realizing I had nothing on my person, I was going to have to change before going anywhere.

"I'll clean up and get the car ready."

"I got myself into this mess, this is something I need to do alone. I don't want to drag you into any more than you already have been."

"That wasn't a question Charlie. You've left me out of this so far and we see where that got you. I'm coming, there isn't a damn thing you can do about it."

"Listen Elizabeth, I don't know what's going to happen when I confront him."

"Get changed, I'll be in the car," Liz said, pointing her finger towards the garage. "I'm leaving in five minutes, with or without you."

There was no arguing. I ran up the stairs, feeling more fully awake now even without my morning coffee. I was fearful, but the adrenaline felt like lightning in my joints. After throwing on the first shirt and jeans that caught my eye I was back downstairs. The smell of burnt pancakes stuck with me the entire way to Mendelium Tower.

We approached the building, moving through the crowds of people funneling in the same direction. I'd been to so many press conferences before, but something felt different this time. There was a tense mood emanating from the crowd around me, and there were more people than I was used to. There were young couples, even laughing children running around the snowy ground. Their joy was a stark contrast from the cold stares of their parents. Did I impact all these people somehow? Seeing the looks on their faces brought in the sharp reality. *This was my fault.*

Liz looked at me nervously, as we weaved in between families. People packed into the square in front of Mendelium Tower, wrapping around the giant granite fountain in the middle, nearly all the benches full even though it was cold outside today. The same group of Template protesters stood among the crowd; their glares more self-satisfied than usual.

"Afternoon Li," I said after Liz and I had eased our way up through the crowd and to the security checkpoint. "You don't normally work the weekend, do you?"

"I'm not happy about it," he said between short and choppy breaths. "Hey! No, you wait in that line." He shouted at a younger man with a camera attempting to bypass security.

"We can leave you alone, you're busy."

"No, no, I'm sorry," he muttered, "I was looking forward to a day of relaxation, just me and a puzzle."

"We weren't expecting to be here either," Liz said, adding extra warmth in her voice.

"We had to hurry down here; we've got to talk with Gerhard before he speaks. It's urgent."

"Say no more," he said. He guided us to the front of the line and pointed at the scanner.

"These two need to go through next." He yelled over to one of the female security guards. "That's as far as I can take you. Hope your day is better than mine Charlie."

"Thanks, Li." I smiled. *Not a chance in hell it's going to be.*

The crowds inside were worse than those outside. With some nudging, and with Liz's hand tight in my own, we made it to the giant glass elevator against the back wall.

"Elevator is closed," I heard a familiar voice saying over the chatter of the crowd. Hayes welcomed us with a frustrated smile, as we nudged ourselves through the crowd.

"Hayes, we need to get upstairs," I said with an urgency I could no longer hide. There were so many people, so many lives I might have ruined.

"You heard what I told the rest."

"This is an emergency. We need to speak with Gerhard as soon as possible."

"Well," he said, eyeing the elevator. "I have strict orders. No one comes up."

"Dammit," I breathed to Liz.

"But… I can give you a card to access one of the staff elevators." Hayes fumbled through his pocket through jingling keys and grabbed a wallet. "You have to promise me you'll bring this back as soon as you make it back down."

"I promise."

"Head back towards the stairwell, take a left and follow it down to the end. Can't miss it."

"Thanks so much, Hayes" I said, hoping the smile I flashed didn't seem too forced. We cut through one of the staff exits, Liz's hand still in mine. I dragged her along, but didn't for a second think to let go, it was comforting to have her with me. Anything that happened today would be my own fault, but at least I wouldn't be alone when I faced it. We got to the staff elevator, scanned the card, and stepped in.

Liz reached out her hand and placed it gently on my back. The tics were coming in strong, my eyes blinking so rapidly it seemed like the elevator had strobe lights as we ascended. The elevator doors opened and we stepped into Gerhard's expansive entry. Anthony sat at the desk; his head darted up immediately shooting us a glare.

"What are you doing here?" he yelled, standing up and putting himself in between us and Gerhard's office.

"Not even trying to put on a happy face today, are we?" I asked.

Anthony glared back at me standing in place.

"We came to speak with Gerhard," I said.

"No. Absolutely not," Anthony said, rooting his feet in place.

"Yes... we are," I said again, continuing to walk.

"Stop," he said, voice quivering. "He's asked for no one to come in. No exceptions."

I continued walking towards the door and past him towards the large wooden door to enter Gerhard's office.

"Stop!" Anthony yelled. He ran across covering the space between us in a second, placing his back towards the door, his arms stretched out.

"Charlie..." I heard Liz's concerned voice say behind me.

"I'm going in, Anthony."

He shoved me in the chest, taking me by surprise and I stumbled backwards. I sprang back and pressed him up against the wall, my forearm caught underneath his chin, it dug into his neck with the entire force of my body behind it. I watched the fire in his eyes now from inches away. Feeling his panicked breath on my arm. My face close to his as I pressed him against the wall, "You are going to get the hell out of my way right now, do we have an understanding?"

I kept my arm at his throat, letting him simmer a little bit before letting him go.

"Stop it!" Liz shouted from behind me, "Charlie!"

I slowly let off, never taking my eyes off his. Then I shoved him off to the side, and in three strides I was through the door. I pushed it open too hard with adrenaline still rushing through me. It smashed against the wall, knocking something from one of the bookshelves at the side of the office. It crashed onto the ground shattering in front of me. Gerhard spoke to his computer across the room, "...I suppose that's as good a place to wrap up as any. It's truly been my pleasure, and I wish you the best." The light dimmed on his face, as the screen powered down.

"Quite the timing you have Charlie. I was in the middle of an important conversation."

"I think they'll be fine," I said, starting to stride across the lengthy room.

"You look like you have something on your mind... Oh and hello Liz, pleasure to see you again."

Liz smiled from the door, Anthony piped up from beside her, rubbing his hand over his neck, "It's time Gerhard."

Gerhard closed his laptop pulling out a memory card. He gave a quick nod and rolled straight past me, handing the memory card to Anthony as he passed. He locked eyes with him for a moment, "Thank you Tony, make sure this finds the right hands." He continued to roll pass him and out the door.

"This is going to have to be a roll and talk situation Charlie. I'm late as it is."

Liz gave him a kind smile as he walked straight past her. I hurried to catch up with him, cutting straight past Anthony.

"I wanted to talk, just you and me."

"Well, that isn't a luxury the two of us have." He said still rolling, fixing his collar, and running his hand over his shirt checking for anything out of place. The group of us came to the elevator and he pressed the button. The doors swung open immediately, no Hayes and no other people. It had been sitting here waiting the entire time. He was about to make one hell of an entrance.

"This is a trip I was meant to take alone," He stood there thinking for a moment, "Anthony, why don't you take Liz down the service elevator, Charlie and I will ride down together."

"Yes sir," Anthony said, still wearing a glare and looking annoyed with Gerhard, but there was something else underneath his gaze.

He got in, and I stood next to him. Liz gave me an encouraging smile, the large glass doors shut in front of us.

CHAPTER 33

FIVE MONTHS EARLIER

Tourette's syndrome will be removed in the next revision. I knew from the moment I heard those words leave Gerhard's mouth I needed to act.

They struck a chord, bringing to life a side of myself I'd forgotten. How could I be silent? A tide was rising inside me, I didn't hold the importance many of the board members did, but a single broken cog could bring down an entire machine.

I had to confront him. There was so much bottled up when I approached, I resented him for putting GeniSense into the grave. *That was in the past.* Resentment wouldn't serve me, I had to channel a more confident side of myself.

He was surrounded by a crowd. Members of the board and press alike, each of them competing for Gerhard's ear. For him I imagined it was a routine day, announcing the next phase of the Template. But my entire self-worth hung on this moment. The trajectory of my life could change here and now. So often I was ignorant to my own desires and emotions, but this one enveloped my entire body. An idea so strong it willed my feet to walk across the room towards the intimidating crippled man. The eyes of the group turned to me as I stepped into proximity.

"Gerhard," I said, stumbling over my own feet.

"Charlie," he said, rotating in his chair and giving me his attention. The onlookers gazed at me with frustration, yet another person to compete with them for the most powerful man in the room's time. He remembered my name at least, that was a good start.

"I need to speak with you…"

I expected reprehension, but he looked open to what I had to say. Hopefully, I could put it into words. He nodded and gestured for me to continue.

"I… I think removing Tourette's syndrome in the revision is shortsighted."

He stared at me for a moment before responding, "Our users disagree with you, the vote for removal won in a landslide. Its connections to ADHD, OCD, and learning disorders are strong. As a whole, it is leaving children lagging behind in school. We've finally been able to catalogue the syndrome's genetic profile; we've proven there are negligible downsides in its removal. It's simply too clear."

My heart pounded in my chest. I so rarely spoke about my condition, even with those close to me, they could see what I was, what use was discussing it? But I'd made up my mind before walking over here. My father's words echoed through my head. *People will tell you you're different. They will say you have a disability, but they're wrong.* I had to be brave, if not for myself then for him. The words slid out of my mouth before I was fully conscious what was happening. "It didn't feel that way for me."

He looked at me for another few seconds, though it felt like minutes. The words of the background conversations lost on me, the only thing that mattered was the look on his face and the next words that came out of his mouth.

"What are you saying?"

"I have Tourette's syndrome, and I don't consider it to be a disability. It has shaped everything about me. The man that stands in front of you is better for having it, and I disagree with removing it from the Template."

He continued staring. Those eyes bore into me so hard I felt like he could see the thoughts racing through my head.

"Life is built from challenges," he said, his focus squarely on me. "I believe those of us who have endured those challenges are required to share our gifts with the world. No matter how much opposition we may face."

His entire demeanor had changed, the eyes of everyone around him now glued to me.

"Do you feel strongly about this?" he asked.

"Extremely."

"Strongly enough to present an argument to myself and the board?"

"Yes."

"Then it will happen. We'll set something up and you can present."

He nodded at me and turned away. It was over, but at the same time just beginning.

CHAPTER 34

―――――

"What in the hell!" I shouted as soon as the doors shut. "What's going on?"

He closed his eyes and sighed. "That is not the way this conversation is going to go Charlie. We have only moments—listen."

The floors flashed past as he spoke.

"I promised you I would pull my weight in this plan, did I not?"

I nodded.

"That is precisely what is about to happen, in a few minutes I will resolve all of your concerns. Your hands will be clean, and James will be released. I'm going to take full responsibility—"

"James thinks he was framed," I said, cutting in.

"He was," he said grabbing my hand, "I want to thank you Charlie. For everything you've helped me with and for making me feel less alienated. You and I changed the world. We did it. I could never have done any of this without you, I owe you a debt of gratitude, without you speaking your mind I never would've taken this leap."

He took his good hand off my arm and the elevator slid into the glass enclosure in the giant first floor. The thousands of people crammed into the entry of Mendelium Tower craned their necks as we descended the gigantic glass tube into the belly of the building.

The doors opened and flashing cameras lit the room, Gerhard smiled and waved as he rolled through the crowd. We split. Him moving toward the podium and me taking a spot in the giant mob of people I felt so guilty to be a part of. A family stood a couple rows behind me, a pregnant mother with her two daughters, what could this mean for them? A mistake I'd made could ripple across their lives in a way I'd never intended.

He rolled up the ramp, cameras flashing all around, he approached the podium, waving once more, the crowd slowly settled. He wore the same face he normally did for public appearances, but there was a tension in the air I'd never felt before.

"Welcome," he said sternly, letting his words extend over the massive crowd. "We are here today because of allegations brought towards Mendelium; our name slandered by the public before we've had an opportunity to defend ourselves. A couple of children will be born naturally and all of civilization skids to a halt."

The murmuring in the room fell to silence. The shuffling feet on the floor stopped.

"We take our technology for granted. We warp the way we evolve as a species, dissecting the futures of our children and our children's children. Historically we've had a near-zero failure rate. Today that comes to a close, but more importantly, today is the day something else begins. Life is built from challenges. Those with the most difficult beginnings may start slow, but in the end, it is they who succeed. We grow weak as individuals and weak as a society. Millions of ancestors before us lived with an unbreakable will to endure, each armed with a fortitude we can barely imagine today. To them death and destruction was just another part of their routine. Overcoming hardship and disadvantage was a daily occurrence.

"We've stolen that opportunity from our children. Not only are their lives filled with unnecessary comforts, the wealthiest people in society now start ahead of the poor not just financially, but genetically. No more disadvantages. No more learning the will to overcome imperfections. These lessons are stripped away every day from the exact group that most needs to learn them. Despite their lack of genetic disease our ruling class is growing weaker and softer with each passing year.

"I will not coddle this next generation; they won't be as soft as the one before it. The allegations are true ladies and gentlemen, but they do not do my work justice. This is my gift to the world. I have made the decision the rest of you are too blind to see."

Gerhard looked across the crowd and paused. The sounds of people moving and talking stopped, the normal background noise of the crowd absent.

"Is this not the answer you came here for today?" he commanded. "You came looking for blame. You've now found it."

He outstretched his arms, one longer than the other, solemnly scanning the crowd. There was only silence.

"I want to tell you the story of Gerhard. Not the one standing before you today, the one my parents named me after.

"Richard and Lina Kretschmar gave birth to a severely disabled baby boy who they named Gerhard. Born blind and with only a single arm and a single leg. Naturally Richard and Lina were distraught. If Gerhard had been born somewhere else or to someone else, his story might have ended differently. But Gerhard was born in Pomssen, a small village in Germany. The year—1939.

"Richard and Lina believed in the ideals of genetic purity espoused by their Führer. At five months old Richard took his son to a pediatrician and asked for Gerhard to be 'put to sleep.' The Nazi's beliefs were not yet widespread, the pediatrician informed him it would be illegal. So, the Kretschmar's did what any good Nazi would do, they wrote directly to Adolf Hitler.

"Hitler summoned his personal physician, Karl Brandt, and authorized him to euthanize Gerhard. The Pomssen church record says Gerhard died of alleged 'heart weakness' on the 25th of July. Gerhard's death was the first of its kind, but not for long. A euthanasia program had been in the works for months and the murder of Gerhard Kretschmar was the first link beginning a chain of death unlike the world had ever seen. His death marked the start of one of the most heinous programs of World War 2—the mass murder of the mentally and physically disabled. Later known as Aktion T4, the program was the start down the slippery slope towards genocide.

"The Nazi party would go on to make sterilization mandatory for anyone suffering from hereditary conditions, seeking to create a purer national gene pool. By 1941 they identified over 5,000 children murdered with the blessings of the state. It all started with Gerhard, the first domino that set off a genocide. My late father chose to name me in his honor.

"My entire life I've grappled with my namesake. I felt compelled to change the world and prevent people from going through the pain myself and Gerhard had to endure. It drew me towards genetic research, it was the sort of idea that wouldn't leave my mind no matter how much I wanted it to. Pursuing it became my nature. But my mind has changed.

"I built this entire company because of my disadvantages. From the day I was born I faced challenges, doing the kinds of things the rest of you take for granted in your daily lives. I learned life lessons in my childhood most will never face. I spent my whole life chasing a way to fix myself, looking for ways to alleviate my suffering. When I finally found those answers, I came to realize it was the suffering itself that created me.

"I'm not alone. Some of the most influential people in our history books faced impossible odds, disadvantages they should never have overcome. But they did. These things did not hinder them, it *made them*. It is because of disadvantages humanity thrives. More than anything else, struggle is built into our DNA.

"I commend society in trying to remove these defects from our children. It comes from a place of love, but we have divorced ourselves from a simple truth. Nature is beautiful, but it is not kind. We see Nazi Germany as an atrocity, but was their end goal so different from ours? With each new generation, the Template becomes more refined. Each passing year another step towards genetic purity."

He paused; a rumble of questions overtook the room. Shouts erupted from all around me as the press grew frenzied. Questions came in the form of panicked screams as the crowd lost its composure.

"I've done precisely what evolution predetermined," he said, now yelling into the microphone. His voice crashing over the crowd. "I've done what my namesake would have wanted. We are different, but that doesn't make us wrong, our differences are a gift to the world. The Template is no more. Your children will be born as nature intended for them to be, beautifully disadvantaged."

Gerhard leaned back in his chair and closed his eyes for a long moment.

"How much different would the world be if Gerhard lived? What might he have contributed to society? He never received the one thing every person deserves: a choice.

"I've made my choice." He said, his chin held high.

"There are people in the world who don't want you to hear these ideas. There are systems, some I've helped to create, built to profit from your fear of genetic differences. But it is precisely these differences that all beauty in the world is rooted in. The final flaw of humankind will not be some genetic imperfection, but rather our inability to accept the value of adversity."

He paused, staring out towards the back of the room, thousands of people in the crowd silent, waiting patiently on his next words. They never came. The top of his head burst open, as the sound of a gunshot reverberated through the room.

CHAPTER 35

———

The floor vibrated, everyone in the crowd scrambled toward an exit. At first, I thought it was in my head, but the entire room shook beneath my feet. Noise didn't register in my ears, my eyes still glued to Gerhard's empty wheelchair. I moved through the crowd, but it wasn't conscious, all physical sensations switched off. I walked closer to his body; the edges of my vision black.

Why didn't he tell me? The man I'd grown so close to had held more secrets than I'd ever known. I had so many questions, questions that would never be answered.

I couldn't stare at him, at least not for long. Right in front of me was a chunk of something covered in blood. It didn't fit into my framework for what compromised a human. The face I'd been speaking to moments ago had a gaping hole, jaw hanging loosely off towards his shoulder. A hand grasped my arm.

"What are you doing?" Liz asked, her pupils filled with shock and heavy tears welling up beneath her eyes. There was no waiting for an answer, she tugged my arm and dragged me through the crowded room and into the back hallway. Her cheeks flushed, she looked out of breath. I embraced her in my arms. The vibrations worsened. I thought it was the shock of the crowd, but there was something else happening below us.

"We need to get out of here. Now."

"You're not going anywhere," said an unwavering voice from behind. Anthony approached us with urgency. "You need to come with me."

He reached his arm out toward Liz's wrist, she jerked away. "Absolutely not."

"I'm not asking you nicely," he said, pulling out a revolver from the pocket of his suit coat. "I will not harm you Elizabeth, but I will put a bullet in your husband's kneecap if you both don't comply immediately. I was told not to use force, but it's been a long fucking day, and my jaw still hurts."

"Did you do this?" I asked while I showed him the palms of my hands. Liz did the same.

Anthony pointed the gun at my left knee. He gave me a stern look. The image of Gerhard's head spilling out in front of me kept running through my mind, that was enough violence for one day. "Fine, we'll come."

He led us through one of the back hallways. With the crowds running out of the building these halls were empty. The freight elevator crept upwards, the buttons flickering as we passed their respective floors. The rumbling had stopped now that we were in the elevator. *What was happening below?* We must have been the only ones going higher into a building that felt like it was on the verge of collapse. There was no noise outside of the cables pulling us slowly upward, further into Mendelium Tower, away from safety and away from reality.

My head was swimming in thoughts. *Gerhard is dead.* He'd manipulated me, he'd used me to fulfill a plan of his own, lying and deceiving the entire time. Liz and I's life hung in Anthony's hands. I began to imagine ways to take advantage of him, calculating the risks involved in fighting the weapon away from him.

"Off," Anthony demanded as the three of us arrived again on the 100th floor, followed by Anthony pointing a gun at our backs. Even his stride had changed, there was a confidence there, precision.

We walked around his desk and Anthony gestured for us to sit.

"We need to get out of here!" Liz yelled, "the building is going to collapse."

"We are perfectly safe," Anthony said, "the server room won't be, but there is no risk for the rest of us"

There was a long pause. He looked between Liz and me, judging us like he'd never seen us before.

"This wasn't part of the plan," Anthony said, running his hands down his long face. "He insisted that you know everything, but things moved so fast today there wasn't a chance. He planned to keep you in the dark but made me promise I would give you a message."

He chewed on the side of his mouth and looked out towards the windows. "I cared about him; you know. I thought of him as a mentor. Sure, I was his assistant, but the man had a way about him, a confidence that felt empowering to be nearby. I owe him everything. So when he asked me for help—I didn't hesitate."

His eyes grew red, and his hand continued cupping his face. "I'm sorry... Even though I knew this was coming, seeing him lie there on the ground..."

He shook his head, tears now flowing from both of his eyes.

"What do you mean you *knew*?" I asked.

"I knew about your trip to the backup servers on the top floor. I knew Gerhard lied to you, giving you a defective version of the Template that you unknowingly distributed to millions of people across the world."

I shook my head. "Why you are telling us this? What it is you want?"

Anthony wiped the tears from his face, he grabbed the gun and thrust it towards me, this time holding it by the barrel. "I'm sorry. I understand you have no reason to trust me, and bringing you up here by gunpoint certainly didn't help that. But I *promised*."

He gestured again with the gun, stock first, I grabbed it. I expected the metal to be cool, but it was warm from Anthony's sweaty palms.

"Take it. Point it at me if you don't trust me. You are in control. I need to share with you what I told him I would, I need to fulfill my last promise."

I looked at him for a long moment, Liz placed her hand on my side.

"I owe you an apology Charlie. You and I haven't had the smoothest start to our relationship, I resented you from the day I met you. Gerhard kept us all in the dark. I thought you were using him, not the other way around."

"What made you think that?"

"His will," he said. "You must know what he intended to give you?"

I shook my head, not dropping eye contact with Anthony. He seemed like a new man in front of me, the marks of my arm into his throat were still there, but his eyes were calm.

He pursed his lips. "Well, you will soon enough."

"What is it then?" Liz asked, any annoyance gone from her voice.

"This was all a part of the plan," he said. "I still don't fully believe what he did was necessary. I can't help but think about Grace."

"All of it? Even… that?" I asked my eyes looking down at the floor, imaging the blood flooding across the stage thousands of feet below us.

"He thought it was the only way. Changing the Template alone would never be enough, people had to understand *why*."

Tears poured down Anthony's face, he fought them pushing through and telling more of the story.

"There was something he always said to me, that it's not enough just to know something. Everyone can memorize a fact or regurgitate someone else's words. It is different to know something as a truth, to actually feel it in your bones. A speech alone can't do that, it has to become more than words."

Anthony looked up through hazy eyes, "And he knew just the way to immortalize it."

He wiped more tears from his eyes and continued, "I argued with him. I think the reason he left me out on so much of the plan is because he knew I would try to stop him. He couldn't let me know until there wasn't enough time for me to do anything about it. Even still I tried...."

"The gun?" I asked gesturing with it in my hand, "Is that why you were carrying?"

"Yes" he nodded, "I didn't know what was going to happen, but I was prepared. He told me he'd planted a shooter in the crowd."

"And James?" I asked again, the thought of my friend jumped into the back of my mind amid all the chaos. With Gerhard dead, the single person capable of getting James off no longer could. "He's innocent, I don't understand why he's involved."

"Well," Anthony began, standing up and collecting himself. "Gerhard's hands were not completely clean. He isn't the type of man who takes another life directly, but his plan didn't come without death."

"No shit."

Anthony flashed the hint of a smile. I began to tell Anthony what we knew about James, his suspicions, and why we believed he didn't commit the crimes. Liz filled in the parts I forgot.

"I'm sorry," he said again. "I don't have the answers you are looking for. I've long suspected Gerhard orchestrated Dave's death, your story confirms my suspicion."

"Dammit," I said, "James doesn't deserve this. He may have made some bad decisions, but he didn't kill Dave."

"I know Gerhard to be a lot of things, but he isn't the sort of man that leaves loose ends."

"I hope for James' sake that's true. I've respected Gerhard for all my professional life, but I'm not sure I can forgive what he's done."

"I'm still grappling with it myself," Anthony said. The three of us sat there for a moment in silence.

"He insisted this was the only way," Anthony said. "But I don't know if I believe him. He lied to me just as he's lied to you. Even still I cared so much for the man.

"He took me in during a challenging time in my life. His own struggles served as motivation for my own. He was more than just a boss to me, but a friend. The world lost a great person today. Gerhard was so kind despite the turmoil that permeated his entire life. I grew so much simply being in his presence."

Anthony paused once again, walking to his desk, and picking up the yellow orchid from it.

"He gave me this as a gift months ago as a sign of our friendship. I'll take it now as I don't think I'll be coming back here again."

"I'm so sorry Anthony," I said, it felt strange apologizing to the man I'd resented for so long.

"I have a promise to fulfill," he said, then lead us through into Gerhard's office. He strode through the room, past the couch and fireplace and towards Gerhard's desk. "That promise also means I leave you here. My message has been received; I hope this gives you clarity."

Anthony took the memory card Gerhard handed him and plugged it into the computer at his desk.

"Don't hate the messenger." He waved over his shoulder and left through the door.

A smiling Gerhard flashed onto the screen. "Hello Charlie. Hello Liz."

CHAPTER 36

———

He wore the same clothes that were now blood-soaked downstairs. The same office we sat in now, his eyes strained but his face lit with his typical enthusiasm.

"We did it!" He threw his single fist into the air and pumped it up and down in a mock cheer. "It was unfortunate it had to end this way, with the incessant lying and scheming, but it had to be done. I used you Charlie—there is no way around it—I saw your passion and stoked it. I saw your lack of direction and I found you one. But I can't give myself all the credit, you were the most important piece in all this. It was your speech, that was the day the pieces fell into place."

It was surreal watching him sitting and speaking right where Liz and I now stood. I still felt him in this office, the trinkets and personality of the long room still existed as a reflection of himself. Seeing his face made it even more difficult to believe he was dead.

"I knew this had to happen," he said, staring straight into the screen. "I recognized someone who saw the world like I do. Society changes all the time, sometimes so slowly we don't recognize it, but something terrible is happening at Mendelium and someone had to stop it."

"You and I are different Charlie, we saw through the facade. Once you have pulled off the blindfold there is no putting it back on again, we saw the truth, then we acted.

"I shared too many of my opinions with Dave, I trusted him more than I should have. I told him how much I agreed with you, that my concerns were no longer in the future, they were here now. My beliefs threatened to topple down everything he'd worked for. He couldn't let that happen.

"Dave was going to expose me. He said the world needed to see that I was insane. I thought the threats were empty, until he showed me the recordings of our conversation. I knew then what I needed to do.

"First I voted in favor of removing Tourette's syndrome with the Template. He put me in a precarious position, I needed to look like I respected his intimidation tactics. Then I hired someone to eliminate my problem, a contractor who could make his death look like an accident. Unfortunately, he made some mistakes, the detectives found traces of the drugs used to kill him alongside his typical cocktail.

"I've already assembled a massive legal team to fight on James' behalf. I've sent them the exact details on the man I'd hired, along with incriminating information about myself. I believe this should be enough to clear James' name. The hired gun, and me who contracted him, will take all of the blame."

Gerhard reached up to his face, rubbing his forehead with his good arm.

"In Dave's stead, I appointed you. It was a gamble, but I saw a part of myself in you. I needed to place you in a position to help me, an excuse for us to consistently meet. It worked. But I want you to know why."

Liz squeezed my outstretched hand. My entire relationship with Gerhard was a lie. I stood up and paced around the office as his recording spoke to us. His voice echoed across the books lining the shelves of the room.

"Blood, drama, and intrigue. There is something rooted deep in our human genome, a carnal interest in these things. People still speculate about the Kennedy assassination, or what might have been if Martin Luther King Jr. wasn't killed in the public eye. Think of the countless artists whose work exploded in popularity immediately following their death. These men live on in a way that wouldn't be possible if they still walked around on the earth today. It's the only way to immortalize my ideas. The mob of protesters outside will explode in numbers now that they think I was assassinated, I'll be made a martyr. I've lived my story, painting a tapestry with my actions. But there is something I want you to know as my life comes to its close."

"I've been wondering if you noticed when you first met Grace. My daughter has autism. Likely one of only children in the country that would technically fall within that diagnosis nowadays. She didn't get it by accident."

His office felt like it shifted in front of me. I could no longer feel the vibrations of the server room being destroyed, but everything in my world felt as though it was shifting beneath my feet.

"I did it myself," he continued. "I wanted her to share some part of me. Selfishly, I wanted her to live life with the same experiences I had, Carmen found the idea offensive. Understandably. But it was the only way I could think of to connect her to me. My condition left me in a state unable to conceive a child of my own, she wouldn't have any part of my DNA, she wouldn't have any part of her father. Would it be so selfish to leave her with *something*?

"Something that would shape her world, an imperfection. I wouldn't have known what to do with a perfect daughter. I lived a broken life, I wanted her to know the pain I felt in some small way. I couldn't leave her with a physical ailment, it would be too obvious, but I could change the way she perceived the world.

"I made a decision, one so heinous thinking back on it inflicts physical pain. There was a part of me that forgot about it, a part that ignored it. For years I held the truth from my wife. Until it grew too large, once Grace reached a certain age there was no more hiding. Carmen was deeply depressed, and for a while, Grace helped. It was another reason I felt I needed to hide the truth from her. I didn't even allow myself to think about it. A part of me knew it would come to a head, Carmen would find out, and when she did it would be disastrous.

"I was a terrible husband, for more reasons than this, I was obsessed with changing the world. The openness I see in the relationship you and Liz share was completely absent in my own. When she found out I had been lying to her for years... that her own daughter was part of the lie, it pushed her over the edge. I found her dead in the bathtub two days later."

He stopped for a moment, the edges of his eyes turning heavy and red.

"It was my fault," he said, voice cracking. "There's no way around it. This isn't a truth I can ignore. But you know what's worse? It's not just a memory in the back of my head, it's in Grace's eyes every time I look at her, when I see her bouncing around the kitchen or playing with her friends, I don't see a daughter. I see a beautiful girl I decided to turn into a science experiment. I see the wife who wanted me to find her dead body. To hurt me like I hurt her."

He placed his face in his hand, tears streaming down. The background sky the same cold blue.

"She is already turning out to be an incredible woman, more brilliant than I ever was. But I simply cannot be the father she deserves. I can't even look at her some days without hating her. I poured myself into work after Carmen's death, I dreaded being at home. No matter what I did the self-hate I felt every time I looked into my daughter's eyes remains constant. I can't drink it away, I can't work it away, and I can't take myself away from my daughter—at least not while I'm alive."

He wiped his tears away pausing again and composing himself.

"I pushed on, for a while. Until I started to make a plan, a way to stage my own death in a traffic accident. No matter how much I wanted to end my own life I couldn't do that to her, I wanted a way out, but it needed to seem like an accident. I wanted to ensure her life without me continued on, that her inheritance wasn't tarnished by my own suicide.

"But then life happened, Charlie, you happened."

"That speech you gave…. It reminded me of what I'd done. But also, *why* I'd done it. I've seen Grace grow; it eats me alive what I did to her. The world needs diverse thinkers, we've refined and refined, breeding out traits we don't fully understand. What if I could change my legacy? I saw a way—to kill two birds with one stone."

I paced across the office and back to Liz, she rested her arm on my own. Her warmth was comforting but still felt miles away as Gerhard spoke on the screen in front of us.

"End my own life, change the world. You and I had our disagreements, maybe you would have come around, I apologize for never giving you a chance. This had to happen, it is a positive thing for the world even though it appears a terrible atrocity. It is something no one would ever choose for themselves, so I took away the choice. My own poor conditions were the gift I never asked for, they are the reason we even have the technology to do the things Mendelium does. I owe it all to my disadvantages, I hope the children of the future will learn this lesson in their own time."

He took a deep breath in and let it out slowly. "This is happening suddenly for you, but it has been slow for me. I've been thinking through how I wanted the world to move on without me. I wrote a will months ago… but I had to make one change. I needed you to hear this story, but there is another reason I wanted to speak with you.

"Grace needs a home. I've gone back and forth on this, but today finally being here has brought a new clarity."

Liz gasped, my stomach dropped.

"This is more than a person should ever ask, but… I don't have anyone else. Charlie, you are one of the few people who might understand the decisions I've made and who has lived through some of the lessons I want her to understand. You've known me in a way most never have, and you Elizabeth have a connection with Grace I've never seen her share with a woman besides her mother."

There was no fear in his eyes, he looked calm and ready.

"I want my daughter to have a good life, I changed my will to give you our home along with enough money to ensure she can live there indefinitely. I don't want her to lose that. I've donated the vast majority of my wealth, and a few others will get some sizable payments. Your friend James, for example, for being put through the wringer, I've hired the best lawyers I could find for him, and in some of these other recordings, I've ensured those lawyers will have a strong case. I've set things right I feel…. I don't have—"

He looked up abruptly, away from the screen. And got a coy smile on his face and wiped away the tears, "Well isn't that some timing. Please consider my offer, Grace deserves the best and I think the two of you are better fit for the job than I ever have been."

There was a loud crash, Gerhard got a big smile on his face and winked into the screen.

"I suppose that's as good a place to wrap up as any. It's truly been my pleasure, and I wish you the best."

The screen went black.

CHAPTER 37

———

"What the hell do we do with *that*?" Liz asked. She walked over to the window and I followed, I suspected panic still raged below, but the city—and its people—still pulsed beneath us. Oblivious to the questions Liz and I couldn't keep from our minds.

"I could use some air."

"I don't think you are likely to get it up here" she said, nodding at the glass walls surrounding us.

"I know Gerhard had a door that opened to the patio." I looked around the office before waiting for her to respond to me. "He told me he had a way out there…"

The office was still lined with too many trinkets on the shelves for me to fumble through. If I knew anything about how eccentric Gerhard was, I had an idea."

"What are you doing?" Liz said leaning against his desk.

I rifled through items on his shelf, eventually finding my mark. Grabbing onto an old geode that didn't have as much dust as the surrounding items. I wiggled it, eventually pulling it forward and releasing a lever. The bookcase clicked then shifted towards us, sliding open and revealing a small ramp with a door out at the end.

"Of course he would have a hidden door." Liz laughed and shook her head. I ducked my head through the door and opened it to the balcony. The cool wind pulled through my hair. We stood on the 100th floor gardens, alone above the city's skyline. The water fountains flowed and the plants bristled with the strong gusts.

"Wow," Liz said as the two of leaned over the railing, below us the sprawling city bustling on with life as much as ever.

"Much better," I said turning to her. "This is too much for me to process at once."

She waited for a few moments, closing her eyes, and letting the sunshine color her skin. "What does your intuition tell you, Charlie?"

"I don't know," I said back. "Gerhard has been manipulating me for months. Now in death, he is still telling me what to do, I need some time to think. There are thousands of people down there, and millions more affected by his decision. My job is gone. Why are we trusting that everything is going to be alright?"

"What reason would he have to lie to us now?"

"Liz, the man has lied to everyone in his life for the last year."

"He's dead Charlie."

"I know, I saw him," I said turning away from the bright reflective glares of the city, "but it doesn't make him any less of a liar. It doesn't make him any less manipulative. He's enforced his will on millions of people today without their consent, are we going to let him do the same thing to us?"

"Charlie," Liz said, touching me on my arm. "What if he was right to manipulate you? You must feel used right now, but you shared the same beliefs. He pushed you to take an action you never would have alone. He was right about Grace too."

"He doesn't get to force this on us Liz, he's guilting us to ensure his daughter has a good life."

"That's not what he's doing?" She said, still holding onto my arm with a light touch. "He respects you, maybe more than anyone else in his life. He's entrusting us with the one thing he cared about more than anything, even though he had a complicated relationship with her there is… was… no one else in the world he loved like Grace."

"No, I suppose that—"

She cut me off, speaking faster now facing me, her eyes wrapped up in my own.

"We are going to give this girl a good life. Something better than she will have otherwise. Maybe we can't be a normal mother and father to her, but she deserves to be loved and I think we can do that."

"How can you make this decision so rashly? With everything happening…"

Her grip intensified on my arm, a heaviness beneath her eyes. "This may have been one of the most confusing days of my life, but there is clarity now because of it. You try to control everything Charlie, life doesn't happen that way. You and Gerhard have more in common than you know. Life is meant to be lived. Would it be such a bad thing to go with the flow, to swim downstream rather than fight the current?"

I had to tug my eyes away from her gaze. Her pupils reflected the clouds drifting between the sun's rays.

"What does your heart tell you?" She asked again.

Why did I have to run from this? She was right, I had the same controlling streak inside of me that defined Gerhard. Manipulating the world around me, forcing distance to allow myself the power that comes with space. That's what Gerhard would have done, never accepting the world for what it was, always wanting to change it.

What was my aversion to change? I kept coming up with excuses for why we couldn't start a family. I'd always imagined we had so much more time, but life can shift so suddenly. Life *is* change, could I embrace that fact and build the life I wanted? An opportunity sat directly in front of us, the kind of moment where life diverges into paths, each with its own risks. Could Liz and I make this work?

Why did I have to overthink this? There was nothing more for me at Mendelium, not after all of this. We could start fresh.

I imagined Liz and Grace together, cooking in the kitchen. Thinking back to the energy Liz had when she spent time with Grace. I thought back to the drawing of a blue bird now hanging from our refrigerator at home. Already Grace had become a small part of our life, she could be more. Would I be the father she deserved? I had so many flaws. Constantly apparent in twitches and blinks, but she never seemed to care. The excuses dissolved, the rational part of my brain wilted. I could see all the decisions of my life spiraling out, the different routes and choices all hinging on this moment. My thoughts felt like code running through a machine, each operation spurring more processes and conditionals flowing through the synapses of my brain. I closed my eyes.

No. This isn't the kind of decision you make by thinking harder.

I turned back towards her, my wife, light blue eyes made more beautiful with the soft red marks surrounding them. The tics melted away. Life was here right now; life was right in front of me.

"Yes."

"Yes?" She asked furrowing her brow.

"Yes," I nodded. My cheeks twinged, watching the happy tears in her eyes began to make mine fill too despite my best efforts to hold it in.

She hugged me so quickly it knocked the air out of my lungs. A cold gust pushed her hair into my face, and I didn't wipe it away, I let it bristle across my eyes in the warmth of her embrace.

I saw Grace and her bobbing head experimenting with new dishes in the kitchen. My mind flashed to Liz dancing around next to her, it flashed to waking up in the morning to find Liz and Grace and the smell of blueberry pancakes sizzling in the kitchen. I imagined having a child of our own, Liz and I building family we'd always wanted. I would get a new job or start a new company, doing the work I loved again without anything holding me down to Mendelium. The emotion and stress of the day fell away from me, with each breath I felt lighter.

This could be—this will be—my life.

We stood there for a long moment together, letting the sun sweep across the sky. For the first time in months, something different happened in my brain. The constant problem solving, the constant watcher of my tics cleared. I embraced Liz in my arms. No thinking about the future, no worries about what might be. I held the woman I loved in my arms and stared out across the city, believing in our future together.

EPILOGUE

ONE AND A HALF
YEARS LATER

A breeze rolled off the lake, cutting through the humid summer air. The scraggly old trees that wrapped the Geller mansion rustled in the wind, their movement so much more welcoming today than when Liz and I first came here for dinner. I stood there, taking it all in, these small moments where some of the only peaceful ones in my entire day.

"Charlie, Charlie!" Grace shouted as she ran across the sprawling green lawn with two friends from school. Her smile was wide, a look of pure excitement that cut right through my fatigue. "Can you play with us on the rope swing?"

I nodded and followed the three girls down towards the lake. It was so nice to see Grace playing with others, there was no talk of her family and no cautious glares from her friends. They were simply children playing and enjoying each other's company. She needed more time like this. She tried to hide it from Liz and I, but I heard her crying at night, I saw how she talked to herself when she walked the grounds. Every small moment like this one was a blessing.

"Charlie!" Liz shouted from the balcony overlooking the back yard. She stood there wearing a blue sundress and a large smile—rocking our son in her arms.

"You've got a visitor!"

James waved at me and gave Liz a hug, then joined me out on the lawn with the girls.

"It's so good being able to see you again."

"Likewise," he said, looking around the massive grounds. "It's a beautiful life you have here, Charlie. I'm happy to see you doing well."

I smiled and looked at him for a moment, walking across the grass and embracing him in a hug.

"You too, James. Every time I see a smile on your face I'm reminded of how far we've both come."

James looked towards Grace and the girls running around in front of us. "It's incredible how a man I barely even knew has impacted the entire trajectory of my life. I sometimes wonder where I would have been without him."

"Me too," I said, as the two of us moved along the path down towards the lake. Past rows of manicured flowers towards the gently splashing waves. "Are you still getting pay outs?"

"Every month," he said, with a tight-lipped smile. "He did exactly as he said. He bankrolled an entire legal team to get me out as quickly as possible, the video evidence with Gerhard and the hired gun was enough to drop the original charges. Now the payouts just seem to keep coming."

"You seem conflicted," I said.

"Don't get me wrong, it's great to receive the financial help, but money given will never feel the same as money earned. Ever since I've been gainfully employed, I've been donating all of the extra he sends. I suspect he thought I would have a more challenging time finding employment after getting out of jail. So, thank you for that."

"No need to thank me," I said, "it wasn't some kind of charity. A wise man once told me that some of the most important moments in history have been conversations. My strengths are in writing the code, but it's impossible to make the impact I want to have on the world without someone who can communicate to others like you can."

"Well, I'm going to thank you anyway C, if you would have told me a life like this was possible when I was in jail, I never would have believed you."

We walked out to the end of the dock as it gently moved with the water of the lake. I turned around and looked up towards the vast Geller estate.

"I'm conflicted too," I said, "something about living here feels wrong. It's everything that Liz and I could ever want. It's even Grace's home. But there is such a big part of him here, it's a constant reminder of what he did to our lives."

"I figured that you of all people might understand his decision, Charlie."

"Understand it, sure, but we were *used* James. He made such an impact on the world; you can still feel the echoes of his final words across society. Every time I tell people I work in genetic tech they question me about the future of humanity and genetic diversity. His scheme worked, but this house is a reminder that you and I were just pawns in his larger plan."

"Do you really think that he planned for you to continue on in the way you have? In a way your new company continues his legacy. He may have opened the worlds eyes to a new problem, but he didn't force you to keep working on it."

"It just seemed right," I said. "You know me James, I have to solve problems. It was the most natural next step, we can never truly know what a genetic variant can do to a species, but why not try to find out? We have the tools. Through computer simulations we can begin to answer life's most challenging questions. We've been able to predict the long-term consequences of gene variants in animal populations, our computer models get closer each day to doing the same for humans. Any problem can be solved if you break it into small enough parts."

James smiled back at me, both stood out at the end of the dock. "You underestimate yourself Charlie, you were no pawn. It's your exact way of thinking that inspired Gerhard. Without you he never would have succeeded. Even after he's gone you continue to build and create things you think will improve the future. People like you prove him right. Your own unique advantages and disadvantages are important to the future of humanity, we need more people like you in the world."

"Thank you, James," I said. "You're a great friend."

"And you are an incredible human being, even though you can't always see it."

Footsteps began to vibrate the dock behind us. Elizabeth stood smiling, holding my son Calvin in her arms. We named him after my father, born happy and healthy without using the Template. I saw Grace playing with her friends, spending some time just being a child. The spires of the castle-like house rose over the forest, reminding me of the man who changed the entire world. I was so fortunate for my life here. So grateful to be surrounded by the family and friends that I love, doing work that would make a difference.

I still ticced, but I barely even noticed. They were just another part of me that I was thankful for, my biggest disadvantage, and the thing that brought all this beauty into my life.

THE END

POSTSCRIPT

Thank you so much for taking the time to read this book. I hope you enjoyed reading it as much as I enjoyed the process of writing it.

This story has been riding around with me for a long time. For my entire life I'd wanted to read a book with a character like me, someone with Tourette's syndrome that, rather than being used as some plot device, actually flourished because of it.

My disadvantages have been a source for good in my own life and I've always craved a story that explored this idea a little more deeply. So I wrote one.

If this book impacted you in any way, I would be extraordinarily grateful if you would leave a review on Amazon or Goodreads. I read each and every one of them, and your words would mean the world to me.

ACKNOWLEDGMENTS

First and foremost I owe a profound thank you to my wife Erin. On top of being an amazing human you've encouraged me countless times through this process. You kept me motivated and supported me through every stage–rereading this novel numerous times to create the story as it exists today. My name may be on the front cover but I know that without you this story would not exist. I love you more than the words on this page could ever describe.

Secondly I want to thank my family. Mom and Dad, with each passing year I am more grateful for all of the lessons you taught me and I realize how fortunate I am to have so much support from the both of you. Mitch, you are an amazing brother and friend. Not only am I grateful to have you in my life, but your own thirst for adventure reminds me to grab my own life by the reins and do the things I care about. Each of you helped to inspire me to write this book.

Thank you to all of my friends. Being surrounded by such a wonderful group of people that I'm able to share so much of my life with is a rare thing to have in this world. I'm grateful every day to have you in my life.

A huge shout out to the entire crew at Fargo Brazilian Jiu Jitsu. Training BJJ has truly changed my life and helped to teach me the discipline and grit required to work on this book every day for the last three years. You are all awesome and training with you all has made every area of my life better.

Thanks to all of my coworkers at Bushel and Roger. Being surrounded by so many exceptionally smart people has helped to elevate my own thinking, and working at a job that emphasizes a work-life balance allowed the time for this book to get written.

And finally, to all of the people who helped me write this book. From all of the beta readers and other authors who shared your advice with me along this journey, it is deeply appreciated. A special thanks to Ivica Jandrijevic for putting together the cover design along with the interior formatting of the book, you helped to make my vision a reality. And finally, to Sarah Karwisch, for reminding me just how special my story was and helping me to clean up all of the rough edges. Your editing truly helped take this book to the next level and I'll be forever grateful.

ABOUT THE AUTHOR

Michael Sullivan is an author and a software engineer currently residing in Fargo, North Dakota. He lives with his wife Erin and their dog Louie.

Outside of writing code and stories, Michael is passionate (i.e. obsessed) about continual education and self improvement. He is a musician, chess player, Brazilian Jiu Jitsu practitioner, and health/fitness enthusiast fascinated with the idea of life-long-learning across multiple domains.

GET IN TOUCH

Finally, if you would like to hear more about the topics and ideas that make up the backbone of this book, or you would like to see what I am up to.

CHECK OUT MY WEBSITE:
michaelrsullivan.com

FOLLOW ME ON INSTAGRAM AT:
https://www.instagram.com/michaelrsullivan1/

OR GET IN TOUCH VIA EMAIL:
michaelrsullivan1@gmail.com

Printed in Great Britain
by Amazon